YORK NOTES

FRANKENSTEIN

MARY SHELLEY

Notes by Glennis Byron

Longman
is an imprint of

PEARSON

York Press

YORK PRESS
322 Old Brompton Road, London SW5 9JH

PEARSON EDUCATION LIMITED
Edinburgh Gate, Harlow,
Essex CM20 2JE, United Kingdom

Associated companies, branches and representatives throughout the world

First published 1998
New edition 2004
This new and fully revised edition 2012

10 9 8 7 6 5 4 3 2

ISBN 978–1–4479–1321–4

Illustration on p. 9 by Neil Gower
Phototypeset by Chat Noir Design, France
Printed in Slovakia by Neografia

CONTENTS

PART FIVE: CONTEXTS AND CRITICAL DEBATES

PART SIX: GRADE BOOSTER

ESSENTIAL STUDY TOOLS

PART ONE: INTRODUCING *FRANKENSTEIN*

HOW TO STUDY *FRANKENSTEIN*

These Notes can be used in a range of ways to help you read, study and (where relevant) revise for your exam or assessment.

READING THE NOVEL

Read the novel once, fairly quickly, for pleasure. This will give you a good sense of the over-arching shape of the narrative, and a good feel for the highs and lows of the action, the pace and tone, and the sequence in which information is withheld or revealed. You could ask yourself:

- How do individual characters change or develop? How do my own responses to them change?
- From whose point of view is the novel told? Does this change or remain the same?
- Are the events presented chronologically, or is the time scheme altered in some way?
- What impression do the locations and settings, such as the Arctic, make on my reading and response to the text?
- What sort of language, style and form am I aware of as the novel progresses? Does Shelley paint detail precisely, or is there deliberate vagueness or ambiguity – or both? Does she use **imagery**, or recurring motifs and **symbols**?

On your second reading, make detailed notes around the key areas highlighted above and within the Assessment Objectives, such as form, language, structure (AO2), links and connections to other texts (AO3) and the context/background for the novel (AO4). These may seem quite demanding, but these Notes will suggest particular elements to explore or jot down.

INTERPRETING OR CRITIQUING THE NOVEL

Although it's not helpful to think in terms of the novel being 'good' or 'bad', you should consider the different ways the novel can be read. How have critics responded to it? Do their views match yours – or do you take a different viewpoint? Are there different ways you can interpret specific events, characters or settings? This is a key aspect in AO3, and it can be helpful to keep a log of your responses and the various perspectives which are expressed both by established critics, but also by classmates, your teacher or other readers.

REFERENCES AND SOURCES

You will be expected to draw on critics' comments, or refer to source information from the period or the present. Make sure you make accurate, clear notes of writers or sources you have used, for example noting down titles of works, authors' names, website addresses, dates, etc. You may not have to reference all these things when you respond to a text, but knowing the source of your information will allow you to go back to it, if need be – and to check its accuracy and relevance.

REVISING FOR AND RESPONDING TO AN ASSESSED TASK OR EXAM QUESTION

The structure and the contents of these Notes are designed to give you the relevant information or ideas you need to answer tasks you have been set. First, work out the key words or ideas from the task (for example, 'form', 'Volume One, Chapter V', 'Victor', etc.), then read the relevant parts of the Notes that relate to these terms or words, selecting what is useful for revision or written response. Then, turn to **Part Six: Grade Booster** for help in formulating your actual response.

FRANKENSTEIN IN CONTEXT

MARY SHELLEY: LIFE AND TIMES

1797	(30 August) Mary Shelley is born in London, the only child of philosopher and political radical William Godwin and pioneering feminist Mary Wollstonecraft, who died ten days after her daughter's birth
1814	Mary begins a relationship with the poet Percy Bysshe Shelley and elopes with him in the summer of this year
1815	Mary gives birth prematurely to a daughter who dies soon afterwards
1816	Mary gives birth to a son, William. Mary and Percy spend the summer on Lake Geneva. The idea for *Frankenstein* comes out of a ghost story competition
1818	*Frankenstein* is published. Jane Austen publishes *Northanger Abbey*
1822	Percy Bysshe Shelley drowns in a boating accident. Mary returns to London
1823	The first theatre adaptation of *Frankenstein* is performed: Richard Brinsley Peake's *Presumption: or, the Fate of Frankenstein*
1831	The revised version of *Frankenstein* is published with a new 'Author's Introduction'
1837	Queen Victoria accedes to the throne
1851	(1 February) Mary dies in London at the age of fifty-three

CHECK THE BOOK **A04**

For a scholarly but also very readable account of Shelley's life and world, see Miranda Seymour's *Mary Shelley* (John Murray, 2000).

CHECK THE BOOK **A04**

Shelley's Ghost: Reshaping the Image of a Literary Family was published to accompany an exhibition at the Bodleian Library in 2011. Drawing on the Bodleian Library's letters, literary manuscripts, rare books and pamphlets, portraits and relics, including Shelley's working notebooks and the original manuscripts of Mary Shelley's *Frankenstein*, Stephen Hebron charts the history of Mary and Percy Shelley and Mary's parents, William Godwin and Mary Wollstonecraft.

FRANKENSTEIN: 1818 AND 1831

Frankenstein was first published anonymously in 1818, with a Preface written by Percy Bysshe Shelley. It was subsequently published in revised form with Mary Shelley's Author's Introduction in 1831. The changes made to the text were not just matters of style, as Shelley claims they were in this Introduction (p. 10). They include the addition of an inner life for Victor which portrays him slightly more sympathetically, the general softening of the characters and the revision of family and blood-ties so that Elizabeth is no longer Victor's first cousin and is much more angelic. The Introduction also attempted to influence the reception of the novel by encouraging the reader to view Victor's crime as a crime against God, something not suggested in the early version. The changes may indicate the differences between the free-thinking nineteen-year-old of 1818 and the mature and conservative woman who revised the novel and wrote the Introduction in 1831.

A LITERARY FAMILY

Mary Shelley's *Frankenstein* frequently reveals the influence of her parents' ideas. Her father, William Godwin (1756–1836), was the author of *An Enquiry Concerning Political Justice* (1793), which condemned all human institutions as corrupt and championed reason as the guide to realising an ideal state. These ideas were published in fictional form in his *Caleb Williams* (1794). Mary Shelley's mother, Mary Wollstonecraft (1759–97), was the author of *A Vindication of the Rights of Woman* (1792) in which she condemned false and excessive **sensibility** and argued for the rights of women to receive a proper rational education.

Mary Shelley's husband, Percy Bysshe Shelley (1792–1822), was one of the major **Romantic** poets and was known for his political radicalism. He abandoned his pregnant first wife, Harriet, to run off with the sixteen-year-old Mary. Harriet drowned herself in the Serpentine in Hyde Park in 1816, and Mary and Percy were subsequently married. Some critics have argued for Percy as a collaborator with Mary on *Frankenstein*, or at least an influential editor.

BIRTH AND DEATH

Childbirth was closely associated with death in Mary Shelley's life. Her own mother, Mary Wollstonecraft, died ten days after Mary's birth. The year after eloping with Percy Shelley, Mary gave birth to a premature daughter who died soon afterwards. A son, William, was born in 1816, and a daughter, Clara, in 1817; both were dead by 1819 when Mary gave birth to Percy Florence Shelley, her only child to survive into adulthood. In 1822, Mary was again pregnant, but she miscarried, losing so much blood that she nearly died.

CHECK THE BOOK A03

For an excellent and accessible introduction to the Gothic, see Sue Chaplin's *Gothic Literature* (2011).

THE RISE OF GOTHIC FICTION

Gothic literature emerged partly in reaction to the Enlightenment, the eighteenth-century championing of the powers of reason, the privileging of science and rejection of superstition. The founding text is generally agreed to be Horace Walpole's *The Castle of Otranto* (1764). In the 1790s, Gothic became primarily associated with, on the one hand, the terror romances of Ann Radcliffe, such as *The Mysteries of Udolpho* (1794), with their beleaguered heroines, mysterious castles and threatening aristocratic villains, and, on the other, with the more violent and horrific reworkings of these romances in fictions like Matthew Lewis's *The Monk* (1796). In these early Gothic works, evil is generally located primarily within an external source, in, for example, such horrifying figures as ghosts and demons, or in such oppressive institutions as the Roman Catholic church as demonised at the time by English Protestantism.

With *Frankenstein*, however, and under the influence of Romanticism, Gothic turns inward, focusing more on the evil within. The haunted castle is replaced by the haunted individual and this leads to the emergence of the **double** as a key Gothic trope: the embodiment of an irreparable division in the human psyche. In this respect, *Frankenstein* looks forward to such later well-known fictions as Oscar Wilde's *The Picture of Dorian Gray* (1890) and Robert Louis Stevenson's *Dr Jekyll and Mr Hyde* (1886).

CHECK THE BOOK A04

Mary Shelley's mother, Mary Wollstonecraft, wrote an unfinished Gothic novel, *Maria, or the Wrongs of Women*, published posthumously in 1798. The story of a woman placed in a mental asylum by her husband, it critiques the institution of marriage in eighteenth-century Britain, and the legal system that gives a married woman no rights.

GOTHIC AS A MODE OF WRITING

The specific conventions of the Gothic have changed over the centuries, responding to different contexts and concerns. Haunted castles give way to haunted houses and hotels; lecherous monks are replaced by mad scientists, serial killers, zombies and so on. Certain motifs nevertheless do tend to persist: the vampire, for example, or ghostly returns, or the monstrous potential of science. More generally, what can be said to remain constant is that Gothic is a mode of writing which, as Sue Chaplin puts it, 'responds in certain diverse yet recognisable ways to the conflicts and anxieties of its historical moment and that is characterised especially by its capacity to represent individual and societal traumas' (Sue Chaplin, *Gothic Literature*, 2011, p. 4). Gothic writers are interested in the breakdown of boundaries and limits and in the exploration of what is forbidden. They are concerned, above all, with transgression and excess.

TRANSGRESSIVE OR CONSERVATIVE?

The Gothic is not in itself necessarily transgressive. It is often more concerned to define and claim possession of the civilised and to throw off, reject, what is seen as the primitive and monstrous **'other'** that threatens the civilised self. That monstrous 'other' may embody a dreadful and yet simultaneously compelling freedom from rules and restraints; boundaries may be threatened or crossed, monstrous desires unleashed. Ultimately, however, in the interests of social and psychic stability, the monstrous is expelled and, sometimes ambiguously, often violently, the systems of repression and restraint are reinstated.

CRITICAL VIEWPOINT A01

'Monsters appear in literary and political writings to signal both a terrible threat to established order and a call to arms that demands the unification and protection of authorised values': see Fred Botting, *Making Monstrous* (1991), p. 51.

THE INFLUENCE OF ROMANTICISM ON SETTING

David Lodge demonstrates the difference between the description of London in *Tom Jones* (1749) and *Oliver Twist* (1838) and notes that the difference is accounted for by the **Romantic** movement, 'which … opened people's eyes to the sublime beauty of landscape and, in due course, to the grim symbolism of cityscapes in the Industrial Age' (Lodge, *The Art of Fiction*, 1993, p. 58). Shelley's *Frankenstein* was written and first published precisely when the changes Lodge notes were taking place, and it was the 'effect of milieu on man' with which Shelley was primarily concerned in her representations of setting.

ENVIRONMENTAL EXTREMES

While some of the events take place in cities – the Frankenstein family home is in Geneva, for example, and Victor goes to university in Ingolstadt – we learn little about these places, and the emphasis is rather upon wilder and less civilised settings: icy desolate landscapes, like the frozen Arctic where Victor encounters Robert Walton, the mountain peaks and glaciers of Switzerland or the wilds of the Scottish highlands and the remotest of the Orkneys where Victor begins to make the monster a mate.

All these spaces are set apart from the normal civilised world. In the Arctic, there is the constant threat from the ice and the obscurity produced by the fog creating a new kind of **Gothic** space: inhuman, cold, isolated. In the Orkneys and on the glacier, environmental conditions repeatedly anticipate the appearance of the monster: thunderstorms and lightening always signify more than themselves. In one sense they come to function in terms of **pathetic fallacy**, with the weather reflecting Victor's internal state and the emergence of the monstrous within.

LANDSCAPES: THE ROMANTIC AND GOTHIC SUBLIME

The natural world is, however, shown as inspiring as well as threatening, or, to put it another way, Shelley alternates between a Romantic **sublime** and a Gothic sublime. To get a basic understanding of these terms, think of the difference between the way the Alps are represented before and after Victor sees the monster or the contrast between Lake Leman in Switzerland and the North Sea off the Orkney islands. The Romantic sublime landscape is awe inspiring and overwhelming in its grandeur, and the observing self is ultimately uplifted and healed. The Gothic sublime landscape, on the other hand, leads to a sickening sense of decline and decay: the observing self experiences only a terrifying sense of disintegration.

STUDY FOCUS: KEY ISSUES `A02`

The key issues in *Frankenstein* include:

- Ambition and the overreacher
- Alienation and isolation
- Family and domestic affections
- Egotism and benevolence
- Healing or threatening nature
- The monstrous and the human
- Sexuality
- The **double** or doppelgänger
- Injustice and society

Keep these issues in mind as you read through the novel because you may be examined on one or a combination of these important ideas.

CONTEXT `A04`

David Caspar Friedrich (1774–1840) is perhaps the greatest of German landscape painters and a contemporary of Mary Shelley. Paintings like *Abbey in the Oakwood* are full of ruined Gothic churches, cemeteries, desolate landscapes and melancholy figures overwhelmed by vast spaces. Friedrich was one of the first to infuse landscape with emotional and **symbolic** qualities. Look out in particular for Friedrich's *The Sea of Ice/The Wreck of Hope* which depicts a ship wrecked by ice on a polar expedition (easily found on the web).

CRITICAL VIEWPOINT `A04`

The Gothic novel, says David Morris, 'pursues a version of the sublime utterly without transcendence. It is a vertiginous and plunging – not a soaring – sublime, which takes us deep within rather than far beyond the human sphere. The eighteenth-century sublime always implied (but managed to restrain) the threat of lost control. Gothic sublimity – by releasing into fiction images and desires long suppressed, deeply hidden, forced into silence – greatly intensifies the dangers of an uncontrollable release from restraint' (David Morris, 'Gothic Sublimity', *New Literary History*, 16, 1985, p. 306).

LOCATIONS IN *FRANKENSTEIN*

The Arctic

Belrive, Geneva

Ingolstadt

The Alps

De Lacey cottage

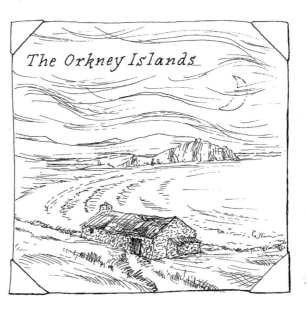

The Orkney Islands

SYNOPSIS

WALTON'S OPENING LETTERS

Frankenstein begins with four letters from a British explorer, Robert Walton, to his sister, Margaret Saville, in England. Although regretting his lack of companionship, Walton writes with enthusiasm of his voyage to the Arctic, and his search to discover both the secret of magnetism and a passage through to the Pacific Ocean. In the last letter, when the ship is nearly surrounded by ice, Walton and his crew see a gigantic being in the shape of a man on a sledge pulled by dogs. Soon after, the ice breaks, the ship is freed, and the following morning they find a man suffering from exhaustion on an ice flow. This is Victor Frankenstein, and he is pursuing the gigantic being they had seen the previous day. Victor is taken on board ship, and, as he is recovering, Walton tells his new friend of his ambitions. Victor decides to tell Walton the story of his own search for knowledge in the hope that Walton will deduce an apt moral from the tale.

CONTEXT **A04**

Polar exploration was a topic of some interest when Shelley first wrote *Frankenstein* with many searching for an open navigable sea across the North Pole to facilitate trade with the Orient. Shelley did not use the **narrative framework** of the meeting with Walton for her first draft in 1816. This scenario may well have been added after she read accounts of failed polar expeditions in articles by Sir John Barrow, Second Secretary to the Admiralty, in the *Quarterly Review* of 1817.

CONTEXT **A04**

Galvanism is the name for the generation of electricity by chemical action, named after Luigi Galvani (1737–98), pioneer in the study of electricity.

VICTOR'S CHILDHOOD AND EDUCATION

Victor begins with an account of his family and his childhood in Geneva. His father, Alphonse, was married late in life to Caroline Beaufort, the daughter of an old friend who died in poverty. Victor describes his tranquil early domestic life and the arrival of Elizabeth Lavenza, a young orphan Caroline finds on one of her many charitable visits. Elizabeth becomes part of the household and Victor's beloved companion. Victor records his early interests first in alchemy and then in galvanism and electricity, and tells of his friendship with Henry Clerval. Elizabeth catches scarlet fever and Caroline is infected while nursing her and dies. Before she dies Caroline expresses her desire that Victor and Elizabeth should marry. Soon after, Victor leaves for the university at Ingolstadt. Inspired by his professor, M. Waldman, Victor returns to his interest in natural philosophy and his experiments lead him to the discovery of the secret of life.

CREATING LIFE

Victor constructs a human form out of dead parts scavenged from graveyards, dissecting rooms and slaughterhouses and, on a dreary night in November, he brings the monster to life. Immediately repulsed by the appearance of what he has created, Victor runs away. He has a dream in which, as he clasps Elizabeth in his arms, she turns into the corpse of his dead mother. He awakens to find the monster holding out his hand, with a grin wrinkling his face. Victor abandons his creation, and experiences both a mental and physical breakdown. His friend Henry Clerval nurses him back to health. The monster seems to have disappeared. Victor receives a letter from his father telling him that his brother William has been murdered. He returns to Geneva and catches sight of the monster: he immediately assumes that the monster is the murderer. It is Justine, however, a servant in the Frankenstein household, who is accused of the crime. Victor remains silent and she is executed. Tormented by guilt, Victor seeks solace in the Alps. Here he meets the monster who insists Victor should hear his side of the story.

THE MONSTER'S TALE

The monster provides a history of his life, starting with an account of his initial confusion at being abandoned in an alien world and the mistreatment he receives from all he meets. He hides in a hovel adjoining the cottage of the De Lacey family: the blind father, the son, Felix, and the daughter, Agatha. They are joined by Safie, an Arabian woman with whom Felix is in love. As they teach Safie, the monster listens and observes and he learns to speak and read. The monster feels great affection for this family, whose story he relates. Believing in their compassion and generosity, he reveals himself to the blind father. The others return unexpectedly and react to the sight of the monster with horror. Felix beats him with a stick and the monster leaves, returning only to burn down the cottage. Lonely and mistreated, the monster becomes violent. He learns the identity of his creator and, out of a desire for revenge, murders Victor's young brother, William, and incriminates Justine for the crime. At this point he promises Victor, whom he accuses of being irresponsible and cruel, that he will disappear and become benevolent once again if Victor will only create a female monster to be his companion.

FEMALE COMPANIONS

Reluctantly, Victor agrees, but, finding the prospect loathsome, delays starting his task. His father suggests Victor should fulfil his mother's final wish and marry Elizabeth, but he leaves for Britain to begin work on the female companion. Clerval accompanies him as far as Perth in Scotland and then Victor proceeds to the Orkneys where he begins to create the female. The companion is nearly finished when he has second thoughts. At this moment Victor sees the monster at his window and tears the female to pieces. The monster, savage with rage, promises to be with Victor on his wedding night. Victor goes out in a small boat to throw the remains of the female into the sea; his boat is blown to Ireland. Here, he is immediately arrested for the murder of Clerval, who has been found strangled on the shore. After spending some time in prison, Victor is found innocent and taken home by his father. He marries Elizabeth, but on their wedding night the monster murders her.

VENGEANCE AND DEATH

Victor devotes himself to the pursuit and destruction of his monster. He follows him through Europe and into Russia and finally to the Arctic Ocean where he is picked up by Walton. Walton's own expedition is abandoned. His ship is released from the ice and the crew insist upon returning home and not risking their lives further. Walton concludes the story by writing to his sister about Victor's death. He finds the monster lamenting over the dead body, and the monster expresses his sorrow at what he has done. He determines to destroy himself by fire amidst the icy wastes of the North Pole, springs from the cabin window and is gone.

GRADE BOOSTER **A02**

Plot summary is necessary for a synopsis, but not when writing an essay. Assume your reader is familiar with the story and always avoid plot summary.

CHECK THE BOOK **A04**

One of the earliest human-made monsters is the golem, a being from Jewish folklore that is created out of clay.

GRADE BOOSTER **A02**

When planning your essay, remember that the most effective discussion rarely follows the book chronologically: structure your essay around issues instead.

AUTHOR'S INTRODUCTION TO THE STANDARD NOVELS EDITION (1831)

SUMMARY

- Mary Shelley provides an account of the origins of *Frankenstein*.
- In the summer of 1816, Mary and her husband, the poet Percy Bysshe Shelley, were neighbours of Lord Byron at the Villa Diodati on Lake Geneva. Since it was a wet summer, they frequently stayed inside and amused themselves with ghost stories.
- Byron proposed that they each write a ghost story.
- Mary Shelley listened to her husband and Byron discussing the principle of life. That night, Shelley had a vision of a man kneeling beside a hideous being which, with some strange engine working upon it, began to stir and show signs of life.
- The next day, Shelley began to write down her 'waking dream' (p. 10).

ANALYSIS

'MY HIDEOUS PROGENY'

In calling her book 'my hideous progeny' (p. 10), Shelley both introduces the theme of parenting and nurturing that will become of some importance to the novel and also makes a clear connection between her book and the monster itself. Like the monster, the book can be seen as stitched together out of miscellaneous parts. This is evident in the way the book is compiled of various **narratives** that refuse to come together into a comfortable whole: Victor's perspective, for example, is quite different from that of his monster. It is also evident in the **intertextual** nature of the novel: that is, *Frankenstein* is constructed out of borrowings from and **allusions** to many other texts, such as Milton's *Paradise Lost* (1667).

DREAMS AND INSPIRATION

It is relatively common for authors of **Gothic** tales to claim that inspiration came from a dream. The first Gothic novel, Horace Walpole's *The Castle of Otranto* (1764), supposedly had its source in a nightmare about a giant hand in armour. When, to move to a more recent example, Stephenie Meyer claims to have been inspired to write *Twilight* (2005) by a dream of a sparkly vampire, she is placing herself within what is now a well-established tradition.

GLOSSARY	
7	**Mazeppa** long poem by Lord Byron, published in 1819, describing the ordeal of a man tied to a demon horse which gallops over continents
7	**Tom of Coventry** the peeping Tom in the legend of Lady Godiva
7	**the tomb of the Capulets** scene of the tragic deaths in Shakespeare's *Romeo and Juliet*
8	**in Sanchean phrase** Sancho Panza is the squire in *Don Quixote* by Miguel de Cervantes (1547–1616); he is given to stating the obvious
8	**The Hindoos** according to Hindu mythology, the elephant which supports the world is Muhapudma, and the tortoise is Chukwa
8	**Columbus and his egg** Columbus, on the occasion when his discovery of America was belittled on the grounds that others had gone there since, challenged the company to balance an egg on one end. When all had failed, Columbus took an egg, cracked it, and let it stand on the broken end; as he demonstrated, it is easy to do anything once one is shown how

---

CHECK THE BOOK **A03**

Another notable Gothic tale to come out of the ghost story competition at the Villa Diodati is John Polidori's *The Vampyre* (1819), usually considered to have established the foundation for the **genre** of vampire fiction.

CONTEXT **A04**

At the time in which Mary Shelley was writing *Frankenstein*, Gothic novels were associated with a popular and 'low' form of culture as opposed to the more intellectually refined poetry of **Romanticism**. Significantly, in her Introduction, Shelley refers to improving herself through talking with her husband, the poet Percy Bysshe Shelley, and his 'far more cultivated mind' (p. 6).

PREFACE (1818)

SUMMARY

- This Preface was written by Percy Bysshe Shelley for the 1818 edition.
- Speaking as though he was the author, he says that developments in science mean the creation of artificial life may become feasible.
- The author of *Frankenstein*, Percy Shelley adds, like all great writers, tries to depict human nature accurately.
- The main intention of the novel is to demonstrate virtue and show the value of the domestic affections.
- He concludes with a version of the origins of the novel in the ghost story competition.

ANALYSIS

THE DOMESTIC AFFECTIONS

The reference to 'domestic affection' (p. 12) introduces one of the main themes of the novel. There was a growing cult of domesticity in the late eighteenth and early nineteenth centuries which involved an idealisation of family life. One's home was seen as a refuge from the world, and there was an emphasis on the affections, the emotions and sympathy with others. This kind of an ideal is based on the separation of workplace and home and the division between male and female activities. Women are associated with the private world and men with the public world. We can see this split in *Frankenstein* with the men working as public servants or scientists, merchants or explorers, and the women remaining in the home, looking after the family as mothers, nurses or servants.

STUDY FOCUS: CREATING LIFE **A04**

The conversation between Byron and Percy Shelley that Mary Shelley recalls in her Introduction is part of a larger debate over what came to be known as the 'life-principle'. Three possibilities for creating life are mentioned. The first is Erasmus Darwin's belief that living organisms could develop from dead matter, known as spontaneous generation. (Erasmus Darwin (1731–1802) was the grandfather of Charles Darwin.) The second is the re-animation of the dead electrically, with the use of a galvanic battery, and the third is the construction of a body out of parts, which would then be animated using some similar technique.

Many of the ideas in the life-principle debate were seen as attacks on Christian beliefs. If humans create life they assume the role of God as creator. And if humans can create life this casts doubt on the existence of the immortal soul. In Genesis, the breath of life God breathes into Adam is what makes man a living soul. The mature Mary Shelley in the Introduction is being careful not to offend religious beliefs when she exclaims that to animate a being must be frightful for it would be to mock the powers of the creator. This offers one possible way of interpreting the novel: Frankenstein's creation is a transgression against God.

GLOSSARY

11	**The Iliad**	Homer's epic poem concerning the Trojan war
11	**the tragic poetry of Greece**	the three main Greek tragedians were Aeschylus (525–456 BC), Sophocles (496–406 BC) and Euripedes (480–406 BC)

GRADE BOOSTER A01

The Introduction and Preface are part of the novel's paratext. The term was coined by literary theorist Gérard Genette, and refers to everything that surrounds or frames the main text. It includes such things as cover art and other illustrations, titles, dedications, **epigraphs**, chronologies, introductions, back matter, advertisements and prefaces. The paratext can influence the reception and interpretation of a book. You should consider how this Preface and Introduction might influence your reading of *Frankenstein*.

CONTEXT A04

Many of the female poets of the early nineteenth century wrote of the domestic affections, and one of the most popular was Felicia Hemans, whose *The Domestic Affections and Other Poems* first appeared in 1812. The most famous – and most **parodied** – poem in this collection is probably 'Casabianca', better known by its first line, 'The boy stood on the burning deck'. Hemans's poems frequently demonstrate the ways in which imperialism leads to the dispersal, and therefore the breakdown, of families.

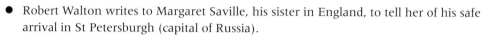

VOLUME ONE, LETTER I

SUMMARY

- Robert Walton writes to Margaret Saville, his sister in England, to tell her of his safe arrival in St Petersburgh (capital of Russia).
- He expresses elation at the prospect of his expedition to the North Pole, and hopes to discover a tropical paradise there.
- Walton recounts the main events in his life so far, including his failure to succeed as a poet, and his subsequent preparation for the hardships of an expedition to the pole.
- He says he is leaving for Archangel within a few weeks where he will hire a ship and engage a crew.

ANALYSIS

ALTRUISM OR AMBITION?

In his character and his ambitions, Walton anticipates or **foreshadows** Victor Frankenstein. As Walton hopes to penetrate the mysteries of the Arctic, so Victor Frankenstein will want to penetrate the secrets of life. Like Victor, Walton rejects a life of domestic ease for a life of adventure and a quest for knowledge. In speaking of his quest to find the Pole, Walton alternates between expressing a desire for personal 'glory' (p. 17) and a desire to confer some 'inestimable benefit ... on all mankind' (p. 16). Victor will later speak in much the same way of his quest to discover the secret of life. In the case of each man, it is useful to consider what might be the underlying drive for their actions: altruism – the desire to promote the happiness and wellbeing of others – or simply personal ambition.

DARKNESS AND LIGHT

'What may not be expected in a country of eternal light?' (p. 15). Always pay close attention to the ways in which 'light' and 'dark' are used in the text. While Walton uses the term here in a literal sense, 'light' also comes to assume **metaphorical** meaning in *Frankenstein*. It is conventionally associated with discovery and knowledge and with 'enlightenment', which both Victor and Walton seek in their different ways. For each man, however, the search for 'light' ultimately leads to darkness.

STUDY FOCUS: FRAME NARRATIVES   **A02**

Frame narratives present another story, or stories, within a story. Shelley begins in the **epistolary** style: that is, Walton's narrative is offered in a series of letters to his sister Margaret Saville (who, interestingly perhaps, shares Mary Shelley's initials). This **narrative** becomes the **frame** in which Victor Frankenstein's narrative is **embedded** and, in turn, Victor Frankenstein's narrative becomes the **frame** for the story at the centre of the novel: the narrative of the monster himself. In addition, there are various shorter narratives, including Elizabeth's letters and the history of the De Lacey family as related by the monster. Another notable frame narrative is Emily Brontë's *Wuthering Heights* (1847), which begins with Lockwood writing about his first meeting with Heathcliff in his diary, and then asking Nelly Dean, the housekeeper, to tell him the story of Heathcliff and the other occupants of the Heights.

VOLUME ONE, LETTER II

SUMMARY

- The second letter from Walton to his sister is written three months later. Now in Archangel, Walton has hired a ship and begun to collect his crew. The weather is still too severe for him to sail.
- Walton expresses his deep need for a sympathetic friend, someone to participate in his joys and sustain him in his sorrows.
- He applauds the courage of his lieutenant who, like Walton himself, is ambitious, and speaks of his ship's master, a gentle man but silent and wholly uneducated.
- Walton quotes from Coleridge's poem, 'The Rime of the Ancient Mariner' (see **Part Five: Literary Background**) in describing his forthcoming voyage to 'the land of mist and snow' (p. 21).

ANALYSIS

ALIENATION

The idea of alienation, which plays a key role throughout the text, is introduced. Walton's ambitions have isolated him from his family and friends and we will find that Victor Frankenstein's ambitions have a similar effect. Alienation is further emphasised by the **intertextual** reference to Coleridge's 'The Rime of the Ancient Mariner' (1798). The mariner's act of shooting the albatross is a crime against nature, separating man from nature so that the mariner remains forever alienated, shunned by his community, an outsider.

STUDY FOCUS: INTERTEXTUALITY — A02

Intertextuality is the term used to describe the way a text borrows from and transforms other texts. *Frankenstein* demonstrates its reliance on intertextuality from the very start, in both its subtitle's reference to a modern Prometheus and its **epigraph** quoting from Milton's *Paradise Lost*. Angela Carter's *The Bloody Chamber* (1979) offers a striking example of intertextuality in the twentieth century. Compare the different ways in which Shelley and Carter use this technique. Shelley, for example, quotes from 'The Rime of the Ancient Mariner' to illuminate her individual characters and their situations, but the **postmodernist** Carter completely reworks and changes 'Little Red Riding Hood' to comment on society and ideologies.

GLOSSARY

20	*keeping*	maintaining a proper relation between the representations of nearer and more distant objects in a picture, basically perspective, harmony
21	*prize-money*	proceeds of the sale of enemy shipping and property captured at sea

KEY QUOTATION: LETTER II — A01

'I desire the company of a man who could sympathise with me; whose eyes would reply to mine', Walton tells his sister, 'I bitterly feel the want of a friend' (p. 19).

Possible interpretations:

- Connects Walton to the monster who himself longs for love and companionship
- The monster will echo Walton when he demands a mate with whom he can live 'in the interchange of those sympathies necessary for my being' (p. 147)

CHECK THE POEM — A03

In Coleridge's 'The Rime of the Ancient Mariner' (1798), the mariner tells of his experiences on a ship locked in ice in the Antarctic. The sailors were visited by an albatross, a great sea bird that seemed to befriend the men. Their luck improved: the ice broke up and a breeze from the south pushed them through the fog. Suddenly and inexplicably, the mariner shot the bird, bringing a curse upon himself and his ship.

CRITICAL VIEWPOINT — A03

The **eco-critic** Jonathan Bate, in *The Song of the Earth* (2000), argues that Walton's voyage through the Arctic is part of a larger colonial project at the time. Walton, he suggests, wants to break through the northern passage in order to encourage British colonisation and trade with the Orient.

VOLUME ONE, LETTER III

SUMMARY

- Walton's third letter, dated 7 July, consists of only a few lines. He has little to report save that he has left Archangel and is now well advanced on his voyage.
- He and his men are in good spirits and not dismayed by the floating sheets of ice that indicate the dangers ahead of them.
- At this point, Walton expresses great confidence in his quest.

ANALYSIS

DOMESTICITY

Walton's **narrative** is addressed to his sister Margaret Saville. She is the **narratee**, and through the letters with which *Frankenstein* begins and ends, Margaret provides our first and our final **image** of domesticity. She even seems to take on a maternal role with respect to Walton, who in Letter II remembers a youth spent under her 'gentle and feminine fosterage' (p. 20) after the early death of their parents. From what we can glean – and we learn very little about her – she does seem to represent, in Percy Shelley's terms, the 'amiableness of domestic affection' (p. 12). But Margaret, along with her husband and children, is given no voice. In this respect she is much like the De Laceys, the family that the monster envies for their closeness. They also may seem to represent domestic bliss, and yet they have no voice of their own: their experiences are represented to us only through the monster.

STUDY FOCUS: THE ARCTIC SUBLIME   A01

Walton's exploration of the Arctic is in part a quest to conquer nature, to penetrate and 'proceed over the untamed yet obedient element' (p. 24). Walton imagines the landscape succumbing to his 'determined heart and resolved will' (p. 24). But nature does not submit to him as easily as he hopes. Like the Alps, the ocean that surrounds *Frankenstein* (it is, after all, where we begin and end) is a **sublime** landscape: associated with something divine, mysterious and immensely powerful, it produces a sense of awe. But the Arctic in *Frankenstein* is also a **Gothic** sublime, with its extremes of landscape and climate. In this early part of his expedition Walton imagines finding a world of eternal sunshine, but he will later come to experience the darkness and solitude that produce only confusion and terror: a Gothic sublime that is anything but therapeutic.

REVISION FOCUS: TASK 1   A02

How far do you agree with this statement?

- Walton is a reliable **narrator**.

Try writing an opening paragraph for an essay based on this discussion point. Set out your arguments clearly.

CHECK THE BOOK A03

In *Northanger Abbey* (1818), published in the same year as *Frankenstein*, Jane Austen frequently **parodies** the language of the sublime. This is particularly notable when Catherine first enters a Bath ballroom with her chaperone Mrs Allen. Austen here makes a **satiric** connection between 'prospects' from a mountain top and 'prospects' for marriage.

VOLUME ONE, LETTER IV

SUMMARY

- Walton's ship is surrounded by fog and trapped in the ice. Walton and his crew see a very large being in a sledge, pulled by dogs.
- The next morning they encounter another man in a sledge, Victor Frankenstein, and take him on board. He refers to the first figure as 'the daemon' (p. 27).
- Walton's affection for his guest grows. He confides his ambitions to his new friend, who says he will tell his own tale to dissuade Walton from continuing his quest.
- Walton decides to record the story so that he can send the manuscript to Margaret.

ANALYSIS

ELOQUENCE

This letter emphasises the admiration and affection that Victor inspires in Walton, who sees great nobility, benevolence and sweetness in this 'divine wanderer' (p. 30). Do we later find these virtues in him? Part of the attraction for Walton seems to lie in Victor's eloquence. He has a voice 'whose varied intonations are soul-subduing music' (p. 30). The monster will be similarly eloquent. Our curiosity is aroused by the violence of Victor's dramatic outburst (p. 29), the **melodramatic** nature of his language, and his reference to 'the daemon'.

DANGEROUS KNOWLEDGE

Victor Frankenstein suggests that the search for knowledge can be dangerous, and he hopes to warn Walton through the telling of his tale. The idea that knowledge is dangerous is something quite deeply embedded in western culture, and stems from the moment in the Bible when Adam and Eve disobeyed God's commandment not to eat from the Tree of Knowledge of Good and Evil and were consequently evicted from Paradise. Knowledge is also often specifically connected with science: the serpent in Milton's *Paradise Lost* addresses the tree as the 'Mother of Science' (Book 9: 680). In the twentieth century, after the creation of Dolly the Sheep, cloning became known as a 'Frankenstein science', and there were fears that what Shelley imagined may well become fact. As you read through *Frankenstein*, consider what might be Shelley's position on the idea that knowledge is dangerous. Is it knowledge that is dangerous or what is done with it?

KEY QUOTATION: LETTER IV | A01

When Walton confides in Frankenstein regarding his ambitions, Victor dramatically responds: 'Hear me – let me reveal my tale, and you will dash the cup from your lips' (p. 29).

Possible interpretations:

- Sets the stage for Frankenstein to tell his own story
- Fits with the idea that each narrator has a purpose in telling his tale
- Suggests ambition or the desire for knowledge is a poison

GLOSSARY

25	**inequalities**	irregularities of surface
26	**ground sea**	a heavy sea with large waves

GRADE BOOSTER | A02

When Walton first sees the monster from half a mile away, he thinks him a 'savage inhabitant of some undiscovered isle' (p. 26). When Frankenstein appears soon after, Walton describes him as 'European' (p. 26) and with a 'cultivated' mind (p. 29). Walton consequently offers us a very straightforward opposition between the primitive and natural and the civilised and cultivated.

CHECK THE BOOK | A03

One of the archetypal seekers after forbidden knowledge is the **eponymous protagonist** of Christopher Marlowe's *Doctor Faustus*, a play first published in 1604.

VOLUME ONE, CHAPTER I

SUMMARY

- Victor begins his story. He tells of his parents' courtship and marriage.
- Victor is born in Naples, and enjoys an affectionate relationship with his parents.
- During one of his mother's charitable visits to the poor, she finds a beautiful orphan, Elizabeth Lavenza. The Frankensteins take her into their home.
- Elizabeth becomes Victor's adored companion.

ANALYSIS

FAMILY AND THE HOME

There is an immediate opposition set up between the public and private worlds, and one of the major themes of this chapter is the importance of the private world (the family) and the need for sympathy and affection. Caroline's father's ruin is, to a large part, due to him cutting himself off from all friends out of pride. The need for others is closely connected to the idea of one's obligations towards others. Alphonse Frankenstein goes to great lengths to find his impoverished friend Beaufort. Caroline is praised for her complete devotion to her ailing father. Then, when she marries Alphonse, he in turn takes care of her, sheltering her from the harshness of the world. The Frankensteins' 'benevolent disposition' (p. 35) means they do much charitable work, and this results in them finding and taking in the orphan child, Elizabeth. And towards Victor they display a 'deep consciousness of what they owed towards the being to which they had given life' (p. 35). All this will become particularly important when Victor later refuses to take care of his 'child'.

STUDY FOCUS: THE IDEALISATION OF WOMEN   A02

Connected to the idealisation of the home is the idealisation of women. Caroline is represented as an ideal of femininity and Elizabeth as her apt pupil. The importance of physical beauty is emphasised. The fair Elizabeth attracts Caroline far more than the other four children in her family, those 'dark-eyed, hardy little vagrants' (p. 36). Her golden hair seems to set a 'crown of distinction on her head' (p. 36). Notice in particular the religious **imagery** that colours Victor's descriptions of Elizabeth, in the use of words like 'celestial' and 'heaven sent' (p. 36). Such language tends to define Elizabeth as a spiritual, rather than a physical being. Fair, beautiful and ethereal, Elizabeth forms a significant contrast with the dark, ugly and emphatically material nature of the monster.

Elizabeth is also seen as an object to be possessed: she is offered to Victor as a 'pretty present' (p. 37), seen as 'a possession of my own' (p. 37). In looking upon Elizabeth as 'mine – mine to protect, love, and cherish' (p. 37), Victor may be taking on a role similar to that assumed by his father, who strives to 'shelter' (p. 35) Caroline, but there is something a little alarming, perhaps, in Victor's repeated insistence on the twice-repeated word 'mine'.

GLOSSARY

33	**syndics**	chief magistrates of Geneva
34	**Reuss**	river flowing through Lucerne
36	**schiavi ognor frementi**	(Italian) 'slaves ever fretting' – a reference to the current Italian unrest under Austrian rule

GRADE BOOSTER   A02

Watch for key points of language you can analyse for AO2. Here, for example, Victor describes himself as a child being guided by a 'silken cord' (p. 35). While Victor paints a picture of an idyllic family life, in retrospect we might see in his choice of words an early hint of the potentially stifling nature of the domestic world. There is certainly some tension here between the softness and ease suggested by 'silken' and the tightness and restraint associated with 'cord'.

CRITICAL VIEWPOINT   A03

Alphonse finds Caroline Beaufort weeping by the coffin of her dead father and he will later have this moment, Caroline in 'an agony of despair' (p. 79), immortalised in a painting. 'This, it would seem', says Kate Ellis, 'was her finest hour' (see 'Monsters in the Garden', 1979, p. 129). Ellis is being slightly tongue in cheek here, and you might want to consider why.

VOLUME ONE, CHAPTER II

SUMMARY

- Victor continues the account of his upbringing. His brother Ernest is born. His close friend, Henry Clerval, is introduced.
- Victor discovers a book written by Cornelius Agrippa, a German alchemist associated with the occult. His father dismisses this as trash and tells him not to read it. Victor disobeys him. He is fired with enthusiasm to find the elixir of life.
- During a thunderstorm Victor witnesses the power of nature. He learns of a new theory concerning electricity.

ANALYSIS

THE MODERN PROMETHEUS

In this chapter we start to understand why the subtitle of the novel identifies Frankenstein as a 'modern Prometheus'. Elizabeth reads poetry and admires nature; Clerval writes tales of enchantment and adventure: both are concerned above all with 'doing good' (p. 40). Victor, on the other hand, has a 'fervent longing to penetrate the secrets of nature' (p. 41). Like Prometheus, Victor is an overreacher. He describes his passion for knowledge as like a mountain river, which gradually gains force until it becomes a torrent that sweeps away all in its path. In using this **simile**, Victor might be said to be distancing himself from any responsibility for the destruction of all his 'hopes and joys' (p. 40).

STUDY FOCUS: ELECTRICITY — A04

In the 1780s, the Italian professor of anatomy Luigi Galvini conducted experiments on animal tissue using a machine that produced electrical sparks. He wrongly concluded that animal tissue contained electricity in a fluid form, but rightly proved that muscles contracted in response to electrical stimulus. His nephew Giovanni Aldini performed various demonstrations for popular audiences in London during the first decade of the nineteenth century in which he applied electrical current to corpses to produce movement, much to the amazement of the crowds.

In this chapter, Victor observes with wonder the effects of electricity on an oak tree. A scientist visiting the Frankenstein family explains a theory he has formed about electricity and galvanism that astonishes Victor even further. Victor does not specify precisely what the spark is that later infuses his monster with life. However, the implication is that electricity is the animating force to be used by this modern Prometheus.

GLOSSARY

39	**heroes of Roncesvalles**	the subject of numerous poems, Roland and Oliver were knights who supposedly died during the defeat of the rearguard of Charlemagne's army at Roncesvalles, in the western Pyrenees
39	**the chivalrous train**	the Crusaders
39	**temperature**	temperament
40	**Thonon**	on the southern French shore of Lake Geneva
41	**Paracelsus**	Theophrastus Bombastus von Hohenheim (1493–1541), a Swiss alchemist
41	**Albertus Magnus**	a German theologian (1193–1280) who studied the brain
41	**tyros**	beginners
42	**elixir of life**	a supposed potion of the alchemist that would indefinitely prolong life

CONTEXT — A03

There are two versions of the Ancient Greek myth of Prometheus. Prometheus either steals fire from the gods and gives it to humankind, subsequently being punished with eternal torment, or he moulds the first human out of clay. The two myths gradually converged and fire becomes the vital principle with which Prometheus animates his clay being.

CONTEXT — A03

The philosopher's stone was a hypothetical substance which the alchemists believed would convert base metal into gold. A twentieth-century novel that draws upon this legend is J. K. Rowling's *Harry Potter and the Philosopher's Stone* (1998).

VOLUME ONE, CHAPTER III

SUMMARY

- Caroline contracts scarlet fever while nursing the afflicted Elizabeth and dies. Her dying wish is that Victor and Elizabeth marry.
- Victor goes to the university of Ingolstadt and meets the professor of natural philosophy, Krempe. He also attends a lecture by Waldman which inspires him to return to his quest to discover the mysteries of creation.

ANALYSIS

BEAUTY AND BEAST

The two lecturers in science that Victor encounters at Ingolstadt are set up in opposition to each other in terms of their features and their voices. Physically, Krempe is squat, with a 'repulsive countenance' and a 'gruff voice' (p. 47). Waldman, on the other hand, has 'an aspect expressive of the greatest benevolence' and his voice, says Victor, is 'the sweetest I had ever heard' (p. 48). This opposition forms part of the general emphasis on the importance of beauty and eloquence. In this society, as the later responses to the monster's ugliness will most clearly demonstrate, appearances are assumed to reflect interior states. Even members of the De Lacey family make assumptions based on appearances.

CONTEXT   A02

In the later eighteenth century, benevolence is often seen as the cardinal virtue. More than sympathy or empathy, benevolence moves outward and transforms through actions. Notice how frequently the term is used in this novel and the characters to whom the term is applied.

STUDY FOCUS: FATE AND DESTINY   A02

The first paragraph in this chapter ends with a reference to an 'omen' (p. 44) of Victor's future misery, and the last paragraph concludes: 'Thus ended a day memorable to me: it decided my future destiny' (p. 50). There are other examples of Victor speaking of his life in terms of fate and destiny. 'Chance' (p. 47) leads him first to the door of M. Krempe, while M. Waldman's inspirational words are words of 'fate' (p. 49). Victor uses such language throughout his narrative and it has at least three different functions. First, in **foreshadowing** future events it produces anticipation and mystery. Second, it might position Victor as a **tragic hero** who is only partly responsible for his own downfall. Alternately it may be interpreted as Victor's attempt to deny responsibility for the misery he causes. Which reading do you find most convincing and why?

GLOSSARY

| 46 | **'old familiar faces'** from 'Old Familiar Faces', a poem by Charles Lamb |
| 49 | **chimera** a fabulous monster made of various parts of different animals; here, the term is used in its more general sense of idle or wild fancies |

VOLUME ONE, CHAPTER IV

SUMMARY

- Victor devotes himself to his studies and does not visit his family for two years.
- He begins to create a frame of a man out of pieces of corpses and hopes at some point to be able to bring the dead to life.
- Victor's obsession isolates him and makes him mentally and physically ill.
- Victor's father writes to express his concern at the lack of communication. Victor interrupts his story twice to tell Walton his error was to reject domestic life.

ANALYSIS

BIRTH AND CREATION

Victor aspires to usurp the roles of both God and women: he imagines producing a 'new species' that would 'bless me as its creator and source' (p. 55). Many 'happy and excellent natures would owe their being to me' (p. 55), he adds, something of an **ironic** statement given the misery he will produce for his monster. There are many **images** of birth in this chapter. His 'workshop of filthy creation' (p. 55), for example, has been read as suggestive of the womb, and he speaks twice of his midnight 'labours' (p. 57). Victor thinks in terms of paternity, however, of being a father claiming the gratitude of his child. This too assumes ironic overtones since his obsession isolates him from family and friends: significantly, he makes no response to the letters he receives from his own father.

GUILT AND PARANOIA

Victor's 'secret toil' (p. 55) comes to seem a shameful and unnatural activity, and by the end of this chapter he is anxious, oppressed and nervous. He shuns the company of others as though he were 'guilty of a crime' (p. 57) – and of course he is: a crime against God and against nature. This is further confirmed in Chapter V when Victor quotes from 'The Rime of the Ancient Mariner' (p. 60).

STUDY FOCUS: LIGHT AND DARK | A02

When Victor speaks of breaking through the bounds of life and death and pouring 'a torrent of light into our dark world' (p. 55), he uses the imagery of light to suggest knowledge as the source of illumination and enlightenment. His discovery of the secret of life is described in similar terms: 'in the midst of this darkness a sudden light broke in upon me' (p. 53). From the start, however, his quest for life leads him to dark places, to death and corruption. 'To examine the causes of life', he claims, 'we must first have recourse to death' (p. 52). Victor also notes that since his father had given him a rational education and not filled his mind with supernatural horrors, 'Darkness had no effect upon my fancy' (p. 52). While Victor here prides himself on his rationality, his activities in graveyards and charnel houses make clear that it is not the irrational, but the rational mind that produces monsters here.

CONTEXT | A04

During the early 1800s there was an increasing demand for corpses to be used in training doctors in anatomy. The law ruled that only the bodies of recently executed criminals could be used, but a limited number of these were available. This led to grave robbing, which became for some a highly lucrative business. The most notorious of these 'body-snatchers' or 'resurrectionists', Burke and Hare, began to murder in order to meet demand.

GLOSSARY

53	**like the Arabian** from the fourth voyage of Sinbad in *The Thousand and One Nights*

VOLUME ONE, CHAPTER V

SUMMARY

- Victor brings the monster to life. He is immediately filled with horror and disgust: the monster appears ugly and unnatural.
- Victor rushes to his bedchamber and falls asleep. He dreams that Elizabeth, as he kisses her, turns into the corpse of his dead mother.
- He awakens and sees, by the light of the moon, the monster stretching out a hand to him. Victor again flees.
- Next day he encounters Henry Clerval who has come to the university to study. Clerval sees he is ill and nurses him through his fever.
- Victor receives a letter from Elizabeth.

CONTEXT **A04**

The word 'scientist' was coined by English philosopher and historian William Whewell in 1833, but the word 'natural philosopher' continued to be used in preference up until the late nineteenth century.

ANALYSIS

HORROR AND TERROR

In 'On the Supernatural in Poetry' (1826), the **Gothic** novelist Ann Radcliffe influentially distinguished between terror, which relies on subtle suggestion to create tension and fear, and horror, which is direct and explicit in its depiction of death, decay and violence. We can still see this distinction today in the different strategies used by, for example, ghostly tales like Alejandro Amenábar's *The Others* (2001) in contrast to those used in any number of violent **slasher** films. Shelley seems to draw alternately upon both horror and terror. Victor's dream would be considered a clear example of horror with its graphic descriptions of decay.

CHECK THE BOOK **A03**

A more up-to-date example of the secret room as Gothic space can be found in Angela Carter's *The Bloody Chamber* (1979). These short stories are full of such secret rooms, including the 'Bluebeard'-inspired murder room of the title story. Carter updates the convention to place more emphasis on these rooms as places associated with transformation.

STUDY FOCUS: GOTHIC SPACE **A02**

Claire Kahane, in a now classic essay, notes that the heroine of an eighteenth-century Gothic novel 'penetrates the obscure recesses of a vast labyrinthean space and discovers a secret room sealed off by its association with death. In this dark, secret center of the Gothic structure, the boundaries of life and death themselves seem confused' (Claire Kahane, 'The Gothic Mirror', 1985, p. 334).

Examine Victor's workshop and determine the extent to which this particular Gothic space could be considered an updating of this earlier **convention**. Compare this room with another Gothic 'secret room' with which you are familiar, such as the oak-panelled bed in Emily Brontë's *Wuthering Heights* (1847). Jane Austen **parodies** the convention in *Northanger Abbey* (1818) with the mysterious suite of rooms that belonged to Mrs Tilney.

DEATH

The French historian Philippe Ariès in *The Hour of our Death* (1981) argues that there was a change in attitudes towards death in the late eighteenth century. In such earlier periods as the Middle Ages, he says, physical mortality was generally seen as a meaningful part of human experience. The increasingly individualistic and secular nature of post-Enlightenment society, however, created a new and growing antipathy towards death. Western culture repressed the material body; that is, society became obsessed with what he called the 'beautiful death', with hiding or denying the physical signs of mortality and decay.

Chapters IV and V reveal much about Victor's attitude towards death. Notice the horror suggested by phrases such as 'the unhallowed damps of the grave' (p. 55), or by the **image** of 'grave-worms crawling' (p. 59) in his mother's shroud in his dream. Victor and his dream form a striking contrast with Heathcliff, in Chapter 29 of *Wuthering Heights*, removing Catherine's coffin lid, and his dream that night of dissolving with her. For Heathcliff, death offers a longed-for obliteration of the division between the self and the **'other'**.

GLOSSARY

59	**Dante** Italian poet (1265–1321), author of *The Divine Comedy*, divided into books focusing on Hell, Purgatory and Paradise
61	**The Vicar of Wakefield** a novel by Oliver Goldsmith (1730–74); the 'schoolmaster' is the Principal of the University of Louvain

KEY QUOTATIONS: VOLUME ONE, CHAPTER V (A01)

Key quotation 1:

After the monster comes to life, Victor dreams of Elizabeth's features changing as he embraces her: 'I thought that I held the corpse of my dead mother in my arms' (p. 59).

Possible interpretations:

- Suggests that Victor has bypassed the normal methods of creation
- Equates sexuality and death
- Offers an example of Shelley's use of horror rather than terror

Key quotation 2:

Victor on the newly made monster: 'the demoniacal corpse to which I had so miserably given life' (p. 59).

Possible interpretations:

- Links to the breakdown of boundaries between life and death
- Suggests the importance of physical beauty
- Shows how Victor makes assumptions about the connection between appearances and inner worth

Other useful quotations:

- Setting the scene for catastrophe: 'It was on a dreary night of November' (p. 58).
- Introduces a motif that will be linked to the monster: 'by the dim and yellow light of the moon' (p. 59).
- Links the language of the supernatural to disturbed psychological states: 'I thought I saw the dreaded spectre glide into the room' (p. 62).

CONTEXT (A04)

One way of masking death in the eighteenth century was through the cultivation of memories of the dead. Mourning jewellery, frequently containing the hair of the dead, became increasingly popular and no longer the preserve of the aristocracy. This was also the age that invented the garden of remembrance, with its idealised statues and quiet leafy walks.

CHECK THE BOOK (A03)

Chaucer's 'The Pardoner's Tale', with its story of the three revellers who vow to find and kill Death, provides one example of medieval attitudes towards death that you can contrast with those found in *Frankenstein*.

EXTENDED COMMENTARY

VOLUME ONE, CHAPTER V PP. 58–9

In this passage we arrive at a climax of horror as Victor describes the moment he has anticipated with increasing anxiety for two years. In much the same manner as the mythic Prometheus animates the man he formed of clay, Victor finally animates the monster that he has constructed out of the fragments of corpses. While Shelley is not clear about how this is accomplished, her description of Darwin's experiments in the

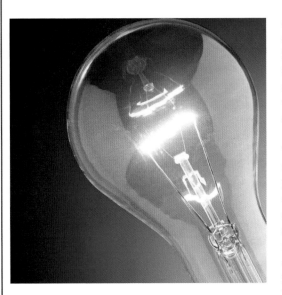

1831 Introduction, along with Victor's early interests, encourage us to deduce that the 'spark' (p. 58) of life for this modern Prometheus is not fire, but electricity. This would certainly fit with the novel's concern with contemporary scientific developments.

The agony of expectation Victor is experiencing at the opening of this passage, the intensity of his feelings, contrasts tellingly with the **atmosphere** of dull misery and dreariness that Shelley creates. When the monster later becomes determined on revenge, his imminent appearance is often heralded by thunder and lightning. The actual moment of his animation is set on a dull and 'dreary' (p. 58) night in November. The rain patters 'dismally' (p. 58); the candle is only just glimmering. There is little sense of 'animation' (p. 59) here. It is an appropriately bleak and depressing scene for the opening of the 'dull yellow eye' (p. 58) of the monster Victor so repeatedly describes as 'miserable' (p. 59) and the cause of his misery.

Victor is immediately horrified by the 'wretch' (p. 58) he has created – and notice how this word is repeated. This is not a triumph but a 'catastrophe' (p. 58). 'I had selected his features as beautiful', Victor tells us, and then exclaims in horror: 'Beautiful! – Great God!' (p. 58). Victor, like all who see the monster, is repelled by and unable to look beyond the physical ugliness, the alien appearance. Shelley offers a criticism of an intolerant and superficial society that places so much emphasis on physical beauty and the importance of not deviating from the norm. That which is ugly or alien is always rejected as monstrous: the exterior is assumed to reflect the inner being. Even little William has already absorbed the prejudices of society and will later react to the monster with as much horror as his brother. Victor's first act, then, is to reject and abandon his child.

Victor runs away, as he so often tries to run away from troubles, and attempts to forget in sleep. However, he is disturbed by the 'wildest dreams' (p. 59). He awakens with a start, displaying all the physical manifestations of fear: his forehead is covered with 'a cold dew' (p. 59) and his teeth chatter. The language here, and in particular the reference to Victor's 'limbs' which 'convulsed' (p. 59), is reminiscent of the language used to describe the monster coming to life, when 'a convulsive motion agitated its limbs' (p. 58). This may be an early indication that the monster is Victor's **double**. Immediately, 'by the dim and yellow light of the moon', Victor sees the 'miserable' monster bent over him (p. 59). This is the first of three occasions when Victor sees the monster by moonlight. The next time will be when he destroys the female monster, and the last time when the monster, in retaliation, murders Elizabeth. The monster, then, through the repetition of this visual **image**, is at the moment of birth immediately linked to death, in particular, to the death of the female.

To the reader, the description of the monster on this particular occasion may seem full of **pathos**. He tries to communicate, muttering 'inarticulate' (p. 59) sounds as he grins at his creator. The first things he desires are contact and affection, and these remain his primary needs. He stretches out one arm towards Victor. This could be a **parody** of Michelangelo's *The Creation of Adam* in the Sistine Chapel. If so, it suggests an **analogy** between Victor and God and the monster and Adam, and anticipates (looks forward to) the many **allusions** to Milton's *Paradise Lost* which subsequently play an important role in shaping the development of the characters. Though there may be something touching in the monster's desire to reach out to his maker, Victor again simply runs away in horror. He finds the monster a threat from which he must escape. Victor repeatedly misinterprets the monster's expressions, seeing aggression where we might see pleasure, affection or a desire to please. He is not, therefore, the most reliable of **narrators**.

In **juxtaposing** Victor's dream with his vision of the monster, Shelley encourages us to consider the possible connections between dream and reality and opens up several possible layers of interpretation. The dream may suggest that to bring the monster to life is equivalent to killing Elizabeth, and in this way the dream is prophetic. This does not, however, account for Elizabeth changing into the corpse of his dead mother. On the

one hand, this hints of unconscious incestuous desires; on the other, we must remember that Victor has just given 'birth' by himself, usurped the role of woman and made her unnecessary. His dream then also appears to suggest that the fulfilment of Victor's 'dream' of finding the secret of life has effectively 'killed' the mother.

These two interpretations indicate the potential results of the creation of the monster. We might also consider, however, what the dream implies about the dreamer himself. Dreams allow things normally kept buried and repressed to come to the surface; these might be socially unacceptable desires or feelings which we are unable to face. And, from a psychoanalytical perspective, the **Gothic** can be said to deal with the return of the repressed, with unconscious energies bursting out from the restraints of the conscious ego. When Victor attempts to kiss Elizabeth she turns into a corpse. This suggests that sexuality revolts and frightens Victor; he associates it with death. He would prefer to find a means of procreation that eliminated sexual activity. If his monster is read as an expression of his sexuality, then it is inevitable that the monster should kill Elizabeth on the wedding night, the moment when Victor can no longer avoid facing up to his sexuality. Since Elizabeth transforms into the corpse of his mother, it is possible to deduce that one of the things which frightens Victor most about his 'monstrous' sexuality is that it includes incestuous desires. The dream reveals what he cannot face and cannot express.

This passage is of particular interest because it allows us to come to some conclusions concerning the nature of Victor's crime. The original Prometheus was punished for presuming to usurp the role of God and create life. This modern Prometheus appears to be punished more for his rejection and abandonment of his creation. Here there are various possible readings of the relationship between creator and creation. We can see Victor as the father figure, the monster as child. Victor might be a new Prometheus, the monster the new man. Victor could be placed in the role of God, and the monster his Adam. The monster could also be seen as the embodiment of Victor's sexuality, which he sees as horrific, perverse and destructive. If it is this which he rejects in horror and represses, then it is inevitable that these sexual desires will not remain buried and ignored. They will emerge with a violent destructive force on his wedding night. The passage therefore provides us with some insight into the nature of terror. Real terror, Shelley suggests, is not a reaction to such physical entities as monsters, ghosts or vampires. Real terror is a reaction to what lies lurking within the darkest corners of the mind.

CONTEXT **A04**

Michelangelo's *The Creation of Adam* (*c*. 1511) is one of the best-known images in the western world. It depicts God with his arm outstretched and his fingers, through which the breath of life is to be imparted, just about to touch those of Adam.

CONTEXT **A03**

Dreams play a significant role within Gothic fictions and often reveal psychological states. Another example would be when the terrified Lockwood dreams of rubbing the wrist of the spectre child on the broken pane until it bleeds in *Wuthering Heights*. It is a moment when his civilised veneer breaks down to reveal something quite as savage as anything he finds at the Heights.

VOLUME ONE, CHAPTER VI

SUMMARY

- Victor receives a letter from Elizabeth. She tells the story of how Justine Moritz came to be a servant in the Frankenstein household.
- Victor describes his convalescence. He cannot bear to think of his scientific studies.
- Victor and Clerval go on a walking tour of the countryside around Ingolstadt and Victor begins to regain a sense of happiness and peace.

ANALYSIS

JUSTINE

Justine's background, with its suggestions of incestuous impulses in her father's fondness and clear evidence of abuse in her mother's dislike, offers a different perspective on family life from that provided by the Frankenstein family. Nevertheless, Justine herself is another idealised woman. She is connected to both Caroline Beaufort and Elizabeth. Like Elizabeth, she is singled out for attention by Caroline and brought into the Frankenstein household, although in Justine's case as a servant. Caroline becomes greatly attached to her, as she did to Elizabeth, and Justine adores her, imitating her in both manner and speech. Indeed, Elizabeth emphasises twice in her letter that Justine continually reminds her of Caroline. A series of very tight connections between the three women creates a sense of mirroring or duplication. These three extreme examples of passive and idealised women are set against the equally extreme examples of masculine egotism found in the novel.

STUDY FOCUS: THERAPEUTIC NATURE — A02

The idea of nature as restorative is important in **Romantic** poetry. In Wordsworth's 'Lines Composed a Few Miles above Tintern Abbey' (1798), for example, the speaker notes how memories of that particular landscape have soothed him in later years, providing 'sensations sweet' and 'tranquil restoration' (lines 27, 30). This same idea of nature as therapeutic is found when Victor and Henry proceed on their walking tour. You might even notice how the language seems to echo 'Tintern Abbey', not only in that Victor is describing a similar experience but also in the choice of such specific words as 'restored' and 'sensations' (p. 71). Victor's happiness in nature will be later echoed by the monster at the end of Volume Two, Chapter IV (p. 118).

Consider Victor's similar responses to nature at some other key moments: after the death of William (p. 76) and after the death of Justine (p. 94). There could be some **irony** in the fact that Victor turns to nature for restoration when his actions have been so eminently unnatural, but notice one very significant qualification: it is specifically '*inanimate* nature' (p. 71, emphasis added) that he claims fills him with delightful sensations. The idyllic descriptions of the 'serene sky and verdant fields' (p. 71) with the sense of the natural world blossoming only increase tension for the reader. While Victor, becoming again a 'happy creature' with 'no sorrow or care' (p. 71), sometimes seems to have forgotten the monster, we have not.

GLOSSARY

66	**Ariosto** Angelica is the princess in *Orlando Furioso* by Ludovico Ariosto (1474–1533)
70	**manly and heroical poetry of Greece and Rome** such as the epics of Homer (*The Iliad* and *The Odyssey*) and Virgil (*The Aeneid*)

CHECK THE BOOK — A03

Mary Shelley's mother, Mary Wollstonecraft, wrote the first great feminist treatise, *A Vindication of the Rights of Woman* (1792), in which she outlines the legal, economic and social position of women in the late eighteenth century and calls for them to be provided with a proper and rational education.

VOLUME ONE, CHAPTER VII

SUMMARY

- Victor receives a letter from his father. His young brother has been murdered.
- Victor begins the journey home and visits the place where William has been killed.
- He catches a glimpse of the monster and is convinced the monster is the murderer.
- Victor returns home to discover Justine has been accused of the crime. He meets Elizabeth, who expresses hope he will prove Justine's innocence.

ANALYSIS

DARK DOUBLES

Here for the first time we directly encounter the idea that the monster may be Victor's **double**, an externalisation of the darker side of his self or a repressed part of his psyche. Even the landscape expresses a sense of duality in this chapter and reflects the emergence of a darker side. At Lausanne, Victor is restored by 'beholding' – and the emphasis on vision is important – the 'calm and heavenly scene' (p. 76) of 'placid' streams, mountains and 'lovely' (p. 76) lake. As he nears home, however, all becomes obscure: night closes in and he can hardly see the 'dark mountains' (p. 76). Now, 'the picture appeared a vast and dim scene of evil' (p. 76) and Victor feels a sense of gloom.

HERE BE MONSTERS

While on one level this can be seen as **pathetic fallacy**, it is also much more than this: in **Gothic** terms it anticipates the emergence of the monster and therefore of Victor's other self. In subsequently going to the place where William was strangled, Victor appears much like a guilt-ridden murderer visiting the scene of his crime. The obscurity and gloom outside Geneva are now replaced by the **sublime** landscapes of Mont Blanc and Jura, still beautiful but now also terrible. Literally, the lightning reveals the figure of the monster; **metaphorically**, it illuminates the darker side of Victor Frankenstein himself.

LANGUAGE AND THE 'OTHER'

Notice how quick Victor is to name and blame 'the filthy daemon' (p. 77), the 'devil' (p. 78), the 'animal' (p. 79) and to decide that the monster's 'delight was in carnage and misery' (p. 78). Here we see in action the way humans create monsters. What Victor is doing is using language to define the monster as **'other'**, to fix a boundary between the human and the demonic or animalistic. There is no evidence for what Victor assumes – the monster is the murderer – but 'the idea was an irresistible proof of the fact' (p. 78).

GLOSSARY		
73	**Plainpalais**	a popular promenade on the outskirts of Geneva
76	**cabriolet**	a light two-wheeled, one-horse carriage
76	**'the palaces of nature'**	from Byron's *Childe Harold's Pilgrimage*
77	**Jura**	mountains along the Franco-Swiss border
78	**Salêve**	Mount Salêve, south and west of Geneva

CONTEXT A04

Given that the novel suggests the monster is the darker double of Frankenstein, it is rather appropriate that one of the most popular misconceptions amongst those who have not read the book is that Frankenstein is the name of the monster.

CONTEXT A04

A 2011 National Theatre interpretation of *Frankenstein* emphasised the idea of the double by having the two leads, Benedict Cumberbatch and Jonny Lee Miller, switching between the roles of Frankenstein and the monster on a nightly basis.

VOLUME ONE, CHAPTER VIII

SUMMARY

- Victor reports on the trial of Justine. The evidence against her appears strong. The picture of Caroline stolen from William has been found in her pocket.
- Elizabeth speaks in her defence at the trial. The court is moved by her speech but only to admire her loyalty. Justine now appears more ungrateful.

ANALYSIS

THE HORROR WITHIN

In earlier **Gothic** fictions, evil is generally located in an external source, in, for example, such horrifying figures as ghosts and demons, or in institutions such as the Catholic church as it is demonised by English Protestantism. This chapter demonstrates one of the main ways in which *Frankenstein* changes Gothic in the early nineteenth century. Rather than locating evil within an external source, Shelley suggests that true horror often lies within, in the mental agonies and torments we inflict upon ourselves or in those darker desires that we repress. Victor sees himself as guilty: 'I bore a hell within me' (p. 89). This will later be echoed by the monster when he burns down the De Lacey home (p. 138). Both echo Satan in Milton's *Paradise Lost*, a work that plays a significant role in the story and has a great deal of influence over the way both Victor and the monster view and represent themselves.

LANGUAGE

Victor's egotism and self-absorption are revealed when he attempts to describe his inner anguish: the 'tortures of the accused did not equal mine' (p. 86). His claim 'I cannot pretend to describe what I then felt' (p. 87) indicates the inadequacy of language to describe inner experience, but is also a common **convention** in the Gothic.

Elizabeth in this chapter begins by relying on the power of language: 'I will melt the stony hearts of your enemies by my tears and prayers' (p. 88) she declares to Justine. Her simple but moving plea to the court, however, has the opposite effect. Justine, on the other hand, knows her protestations of innocence will be unheard and she is persuaded to lie by her confessor in order to obtain absolution: 'he threatened and menaced, until I almost began to think I was the monster that he said I was' (p. 88). Language seems to have power only when combined with other qualities, such as social position.

STUDY FOCUS: SATANIC HEROES A03

The **Romantic** poets read Milton's Satan in *Paradise Lost* as a heroic figure: an ambitious individualist, alienated, outcast, rebelling against authority, bent on revenge and much maligned. William Blake famously said that 'Milton was of the Devil's Party without knowing it'. Such a revisionary reading of Milton is found in William Godwin's *Political Justice*, where Godwin defends Satan's principled opposition to tyranny. Mary Shelley could be said to produce Satanic **protagonists** in both Victor and the monster but their Satanic rebellions are not viewed particularly sympathetically. This is true of some other Satanic protagonists, such as Emily Brontë's Heathcliff, that 'imp of Satan' in *Wuthering Heights*, or the unnamed husband in Angela Carter's *The Bloody Chamber*.

GLOSSARY

87   **the ballots** originally small balls thrown to indicate the choice made by voters

---

CHECK THE BOOK A03

John Milton's *Paradise Lost* is a seventeenth-century epic poem in blank verse that tells the story of the creation of Adam and Eve and how they came to lose their place in Eden. More importantly for the Romantic poets, it also tells the story of Lucifer, an angel in heaven who led his followers in a war against God and was consequently exiled from heaven.

CRITICAL VIEWPOINT A02

In *The Coherence of Gothic Conventions* (Methuen, 1986), Eve Kosofsky Sedgewick discusses the Gothic emphasis on the 'unspeakable', not only in the sense of nameless horrors but also in the **narrative** structure, with its often illegible or incomplete manuscripts and its tendency to place stories within stories, distancing the reader and throwing doubt on the accuracy of what is said.

VOLUME TWO, CHAPTER I

SUMMARY

- Full of guilt, Victor again shuns family and friends. He is tempted by suicide but fears to leave those he loves to the vengeance of the monster.
- Elizabeth has changed, having lost faith in the essential goodness of humankind.
- Victor attempts to forget his sorrows and sets off for the valley of Chamounix.

ANALYSIS

ALIENATION

While Victor's decision not to speak up at Justine's trial may be misguided, he is probably right in assuming no one would believe him anyway. Again, there is a sense of the 'unspeakable' and in this case the unspeakable is clearly the monster itself. Victor's inability to speak, to share his knowledge, is part of a larger sense of his alienation: his isolation from family and friends. Formerly this was produced by his obsessive desire to create, now it is caused by what he has created. He considers suicide, and claims he refrains only because he fears leaving his family and friends exposed 'to the malice of the fiend' (p. 94).

MOTHER NATURE

Victor does leave his family and friends, however, which given his supposed fears for their safety is in itself interesting, and the chapter shows one of his many attempts to forget himself in the magnificence of nature. In the valley of Chamounix he is soothed: 'maternal nature bade me weep no more' (p. 98). Arriving in the village, he is lulled to sleep by the rushing of the river. Here Victor offers a typically Romantic notion of 'Mother Nature'. But the landscape, with its avalanches and the lightning that plays upon Mont Blanc, ultimately seems less designed to soothe than to herald the forthcoming arrival of the monster.

> **CONTEXT**   **A03**
>
> In 'Tintern Abbey', Wordsworth provides one of the best-known depictions of a maternal nature when he describes her as the 'nurse,/ The guide, the guardian of my heart, and soul/ Of all my moral being' (lines 109–11).

STUDY FOCUS: MEN AND MONSTERS   **A02**

Responding to the execution of Justine, Elizabeth says that before she had looked on accounts of vice or injustice as remote stories of 'ancient days', but now 'misery has come home, and men appear to me as monsters thirsting for each other's blood' (p. 95). This is an important statement for two reasons.

First, it suggests one of the ways in which *Frankenstein* itself moves away from the tendency of previous Gothic fictions to set events in far-off times and places associated with barbarism, superstition and torture. *Frankenstein*, set in the late eighteenth century, depicts a world that would seem quite familiar to its first readers, with its interests in such things as polar expeditions, galvinism and the principle of life.

Second, the statement echoes on a wider social level the **doubling** of Victor and the monster. In this respect, Victor's comment that he was 'the only *unquiet thing* that wandered *restless* in a scene so beautiful and heavenly' (p. 94, emphasis added) makes a similar point. Describing himself with language more usually associated with ghosts – 'unquiet', 'restless' – and dehumanising himself as a 'thing', Victor's statement similarly implies that the human here is the monstrous.

GLOSSARY

97	**a type of me**	a prefiguration; more generally, an **image** or figure
95	**aiguilles**	(French) literally, needles – a reference to the sharp peaks of Mont Blanc

VOLUME TWO, CHAPTER II

SUMMARY

- Victor initially receives some comfort from the **sublime** and magnificent natural world, but as the weather changes his gloom returns.
- He climbs to the top of Montanvert where the figure of a man approaches him with superhuman speed. It is the monster.
- Victor rejects him. The monster complains of being abandoned and claims only misery turned him into a fiend.
- The monster's eloquence convinces Victor he should listen. They proceed to a hut where the monster begins to tell his story.

ANALYSIS

MONSTROSITY AND THE VISUAL

The term 'monster' originally referred to something to be shown, something that serves to demonstrate (Latin, *monstrare*: to demonstrate) and to warn (Latin, *monere*: to warn). Early monsters are violations of nature, composed of ill-assorted parts, like the hydra, with too many heads, or the griffin with the head and wings of an eagle combined with the body and paws of a lion. Originally, then, monstrosity is very much a matter of the visual. While on one level, Shelley continues with this tradition, on another level, she questions it, suggesting monstrosity lies within, not without.

The power of the visual, however, is strong, and the monster has learned this lesson well. When Victor cries 'Begone! relieve me from the sight of your detested form' (p. 104), the monster simply places his hands before Victor's eyes. 'Hear my tale' (p. 104), he requests. The reader of the novel, dealing with words, not **images**, cannot see the 'detested form', and is perhaps more willing to hear the tale and more able to grant him compassion.

STUDY FOCUS: TERROR AND OBSCURITY   A01

Ann Radcliffe, one of the first **Gothic** novelists and the author of *The Mysteries of Udolpho* (1794), distinguishes between horror and terror in her essay 'On the Supernatural in Poetry' (1826). Terror, she argues, is characterised by uncertainty and obscurity in its treatment of the 'dreaded evil'.

Obscurity leaves something for the imagination to exaggerate. Horror, on the other hand, is characterised by clear and direct displays of that same 'dreaded evil'. Radcliffe turns to Shakespeare for examples, and finds *Hamlet* a better example of terror than *Macbeth*: the representation of the ghost of Banquo is too immediate and direct – too horrific; the appearance of the ghost of Hamlet's father, on the other hand, is marked by obscurity and a gloomy sense of terror.

In terms of *Frankenstein*, horror clearly characterises Victor's descriptions of his secret workshop and the dream that follows the creation of the being. This particular chapter, however, begins by descriptions of the landscape which emphasise obscurity and uncertainty, and in that way prepare us for the imminent arrival of the monster. Look carefully at the paragraph beginning 'Where had they fled...' (p. 99) and identify some of the words which contribute to this sense of uncertainty.

CRITICAL VIEWPOINT A03

Devendra Varma elaborates on the distinction between terror and horror when he writes that it 'is the difference between awful apprehension and sickening realization: between the smell of death and stumbling against a corpse' (Devendra Varma, *The Gothic Flame*, Russell, 1966, p. 130).

GLOSSARY

99	**presence-chamber**	room in which the sovereign receives guests
100	**Montanvert**	viewpoint above Chamonix
100	**concussion of air**	disturbance of air
101	**'We rest ... mutability!'**	from Percy Shelley's 'Mutability' (1816)
102	**maw**	mouth

EXTENDED COMMENTARY

VOLUME TWO, CHAPTER II PP. 101–3

Tormented by guilt and rage following the deaths of William and Justine, Victor goes to the valley of Chamounix in an attempt to forget his sorrows in the magnificence of nature. On the day of his arrival, he does indeed find comfort amongst the sublime and magnificent scenery. The passage in question describes the contrasting scene on the summit of Montanvert the following day. All has now changed. A storm heralds the imminent arrival of the monster, and nature seems violent and terrifying. Victor sees a large and agile form bounding over the crevices with superhuman speed and knows what he must now face. Unable to respond in his usual manner to the monster

and what he represents (unable, that is, to run away or fall asleep) Victor almost faints. This escape too is denied him by a cold blast of wind. He is forced to accept a confrontation with his monster and resolves to kill him.

The exchange between Victor and the monster is of particular interest for the various shifts in roles that take place. An examination of language reveals the first of these. The monster's language is generally calm and reasoned, biblically solemn and dignified. He is an eloquent **rhetorician**. He draws with skill upon such devices as **oxymoron** and **antithesis**: 'I ought to be thy Adam, but I am rather the fallen angel' (p. 103). His most terrifying threats are expressed with elegantly constructed phrases: 'If you will comply with my conditions, I will leave them and you at peace; but if you refuse, I will glut the maw of death, until it be satiated with the blood of your remaining friends' (p. 102). **Parallelism** and repetition here produce, in contrast to the terrible violence threatened, a harmonious arrangement of words, suggestive of balance and reasoning. This is the first time we hear the monster speak, and we may have been expecting only grunts. What we find, however, is that despite his hideous appearance, he is the most eloquent character in the novel. There is a striking contradiction here between the verbal and the visual. The source of his eloquence and **analogies** only later becomes clear when we learn about his education and the impressive reading list that includes *Paradise Lost*.

In comparison, Victor seems to do little more than splutter insults and threats. His language clearly reveals that he is in the grip of a terrible savage passion, and, of course, this is understandable. But he is ultimately only diminished by this passion. His speeches are almost absurdly **melodramatic**, full of exclamations, and such theatrical expressions as 'Begone, vile insect!' (p. 102); he would appear to have lost all sense of proportion here in referring to the eight-foot high monster as an insect. He addresses the monster in language reminiscent of the vengeful God of the Old Testament: 'do not

GRADE BOOSTER A02

Examiners will expect you to be able to write about the specific techniques and methods used within a text. When you do this, make sure you show how they contribute to the meaning of the text. Instead of just identifying an example of parallelism in the monster's speech, for example, explain the great contrast between what he says – he expresses anger and threatens violence – and how he says it – using the parallelism that suggests calm and reasoned balance.

you fear the fierce vengeance of my arm wreaked on your miserable head?' (p. 102). Victor repeatedly refers to the violence of his feelings: his rage is 'without bounds' (p. 102); he 'trembled with rage and horror' (p. 101); 'rage and hatred' (p. 102) at first deprive him of speech, but then he overwhelms the monster with words 'expressive of furious detestation and contempt' (p. 102). For all Victor's threats, these words convey little more than a sense of flailing impotence. This is further emphasised by the constant references to the superior physical strength and agility of the monster. As he reminds Victor, 'thou hast made me more powerful than thyself' (p.102). When Victor springs upon him in rage, he can easily elude his creator's grasp. Victor may call him an 'insect' (p. 102), but, considering the power and size of the monster, the **image** could be more appropriately applied to Victor himself. Victor claims to detect 'disdain and malignity' (p. 102) in the monster's countenance. In this passage, however, the boundaries between the human and the monstrous seem to dissolve as Victor's savage passions suggest that he, not the apparently more civilised monster, is the true monster.

Variously employing such **epithets** as 'devil', 'daemon' and 'fiend' (p. 102), Victor also places the monster in the role of Satan, claiming the torments of hell are not a sufficient punishment for his crimes. The monster agrees with the **analogy**, but presents it in quite a different light when he describes his miserable condition. Three times in this passage he reminds Victor 'I am thy creature' (pp. 102, 103). He should, therefore, be Adam to Victor's God, but is 'rather the fallen angel' (p. 103). He has been transformed into this 'fallen angel' not through any fault of his own, but because Victor has made him, like Satan, the most miserable of beings. Despite his power and size, the monster believes Victor, as his creator, is still his 'natural lord and king' (pp. 102–3). He describes himself as 'devoted' (p. 102) and is quite willing to be submissive. He insists only that if he is to play his natural and proper role, to be 'mild and docile' (p. 102) to his lord, then Victor must too play his natural and proper role and not simply reject and abandon him. It is only much later, when Victor destroys his last hope by tearing apart his female creation, that the monster abandons his belief in these roles. Addressing Victor as 'Slave', he then assumes authority: 'You are my creator, but I am your master – obey!' (p. 172).

Echoing William Godwin's belief that man's natural emotions were those of benevolence, affection and pity, Shelley has her monster, her natural man or new Adam, claim that he was instinctively 'benevolent and good' (p. 103). What the monster desires is what Victor rejects: love and companionship. While Victor chooses his own isolation, it is forced upon the monster and his resulting misery makes him 'a fiend' (p. 103). Shelley suggests that it is natural to long for affection, and that in this respect, again, it is Victor, not the monster, who is abnormal. Through the repeated confusion and exchange of roles in this passage, the undermining of all our assumptions and expectations, Shelley makes it difficult to claim any straightforward opposition between the human and the monstrous.

CRITICAL VIEWPOINT **A03**

According to Chris Baldick, *Paradise Lost* 'elaborates upon the connections between two kinds of myth: a myth of creation and a myth of transgression. *Frankenstein* does this too, but its sinister travesty collapses the two kinds of myth together so that now creation and transgression appear to be the same thing' (Chris Baldick, *In Frankenstein's Shadow*, 1990, p. 40).

VOLUME TWO, CHAPTER III

SUMMARY

- The monster begins his story.
- He has vague memories of his first consciousness and the discovery of sensations.
- He seeks refuge in a forest and discovers the use of fire, but needs food and shelter. The people he encounters react with fear, and he is driven out of a village.
- He finds a hovel adjoined to a cottage belonging to the De Lacey family and makes this his home.

ANALYSIS

EDUCATION

At the time she was writing *Frankenstein*, Shelley was reading John Locke's *Essay Concerning Human Understanding* (1690), and she applies Locke's theories in describing the education of the monster. Locke describes the child's mind at birth as a *tabula rasa*, a blank slate, and argues that the individual is then formed through experiences. Shelley was also reading Jean-Jacques Rousseau, who offered a secular version of the Fall in arguing that natural man is born in a state of innocence.

The monster in the woods is in many ways like a newly born child, and one of the first things that he has to learn is the concept of difference, to distinguish between his different senses – seeing, feeling, hearing – as well as between the things that he then discovers through the use of those senses, such as pain and pleasure, light and dark. Soon, he will learn the meaning of difference as it applies to himself, something for which he will suffer, and he will be corrupted by his contact with human society.

STUDY FOCUS: POINT OF VIEW   A02

David Lodge claims that 'The choice of the point(s) of view from which the story is told is arguably the most important single decision that the novelist has to make, for it fundamentally affects the way readers will respond, emotionally and morally, to the fictional characters and their actions' (*The Art of Fiction*, 1993, p. 26). Consider the effects of the shift to the monster's **point of view** in this chapter. It could be said to challenge Victor's authority. It also prompts the reader to begin responding with sympathy to the monster's plight. After reading this chapter, consider if there are any other changes in your responses to either Victor or the monster that are caused by this shift in point of view.

MOONLIGHT AS METAPHOR

In classical mythology, the moon is associated with the goddess Diana, while the sun is associated with the god Apollo, and so the moon is often associated with the feminine. If you are familiar with Charlotte Brontë's *Jane Eyre* (1847), you will know that Jane often conflates the moon with the mother. The moon plays a significant role throughout *Frankenstein*, taking on various **symbolic** associations, and at this point the maternal connection seems to predominate. The first thing the motherless monster finds pleasure in is the bright moon, the 'radiant form' (p. 106) upon which he gazes with wonder.

GLOSSARY

108	**Pandaemonium**	the city built in Hell by the fallen angels in *Paradise Lost*

CONTEXT   A04

Stories of feral children – those who grow up in the wild without human contact, sometimes supposedly nurtured by animals – have a long history. In Shelley's time, the most famous case was that of Victor the Wild Boy of Aveyron, found wandering in the woods in France in 1797. He was captured, displayed in the town, and escaped. In 1800, at the age of around 12, he emerged from the woods on his own. Attempts were made to socialise him, but he never managed to learn language.

CHECK THE BOOK   A03

Angela Carter offers a variation on the story of the feral child in 'Wolf-Alice' in *The Bloody Chamber* (1979), where the nuns leave a wild girl they have been unable to civilise in the household of a monstrous vampiric Duke. The girl's development can be usefully compared and contrasted with the development of the monster.

VOLUME TWO, CHAPTER IV

SUMMARY

- The monster begins to learn language from the De Laceys.
- He observes their poverty and tries to help them with their chores.
- Admiring their beauty, he is shocked to view himself in a pool and is filled with shame about what he sees as his deformities.
- The gentleness of the De Laceys leads him to hope they may receive him with kindness.

ANALYSIS

THE MONSTROUS IMAGE

In Milton's *Paradise Lost*, Eve is narcissistically captivated by her own image in a pool. There is no narcissism involved, however, when Shelley rewrites this scene for the monster. Rather, he repeats Victor's earlier response to him, when he starts back in horror. The monster takes the **image** as the reality, the surface as the container of truth, when the reflection convinces him that he is 'the monster that I am' (p. 116). He internalises the view and judgement of society and accepts that definition of his self.

THE ART OF LANGUAGE

At the same time as the monster discovers that he is, visually, monstrous and unnatural, he also discovers language and comes to hope that language can compensate him for his 'miserable deformity' (p. 117). He is filled with hope that his 'gentle demeanour and conciliating words' (p. 118) could offset the disgust the De Laceys would initially feel, and win their love. Consequently, he applies himself to learning 'the art of language' (p. 118).

THE FAMILY

Equally importantly, the monster is learning about the social institution of the family, and about personal relationships. The devotion that the family members show to each other can only function to make him more aware of his isolation, and, for the reader, their affectionate natures contrast strikingly with Victor's abandonment of his 'child'. Notice that once again the mother is absent from this household. We learn nothing about her. And, indeed, once the Arabian Safie arrives, we will find that her mother is dead too.

NATURE

The conclusion of this chapter shows the monster responding in a childlike manner to the natural world, rejoicing in the coming of spring. In his responses to nature, he can be compared to Victor. Nature here again takes on a healing function and in spite of all he has learned about his own isolation and difference, as the birds sing and the plants grow, the monster is filled with 'anticipations of joy' (p. 118).

GLOSSARY

114	**viands** foodstuffs
118	**the ass and the lap-dog** Jean de La Fontaine (1621–95), Fables 4.5. The ass sees the lap-dog petted for fawning on its master, tries the same trick and is beaten

---

CHECK THE FILM A03

The first film adaptation of the novel was the silent black-and-white *Frankenstein* of 1910, directed by J. Searle Dawley. Here the monster sees himself for the first time in a mirror and is terrified by his own image.

CONTEXT A04

The tendency for everyone in the novel to assume that the monster is evil on the basis of his appearance may tie in with the contemporary theories of the eighteenth-century Swiss physiognomist Johan Caspar Lavater (1741–1801). Physiognomy is a pseudo-science arguing that one's character is manifest in one's appearance and that the trained physiognomist can therefore identify a person's moral nature by reading that person's physical characteristics.

CHECK THE FILM A03

In James Whale's *Frankenstein* (1931), the monster's childlike innocence is shown in a scene involving a young girl called Maria. She is unafraid of him and they play together, throwing flowers into the water. When they run out of flowers, he throws her in, expecting that she too will float. He runs away confused and she drowns.

VOLUME TWO, CHAPTER V

SUMMARY

- Safie arrives. The monster listens as she is taught English by the family.
- The monster learns about history, politics and religion and of the cruelty of humankind towards what is alien and different.

ANALYSIS

MONSTROUS REVOLUTION

The monster applies the lessons he learns from Volney's *Ruins of Empires* to his own situation. His identification with those lacking the two most valued possessions, 'high and unsullied descent united with riches' (p. 123), suggests on one level he can be read as representative of the oppressed classes. Some critics have consequently interpreted *Frankenstein* as a commentary on class struggle. More particularly, the class issue combined with the idea of a monster that has gone beyond the control of its creator brings to mind the French Revolution of 1789. Then the crowd or mob was frequently represented as a monster. Shelley, while passionate about the need for justice and reform, was, like most middle-class English people of the time, anxious about the possibility of revolutionary mob violence.

ALIENATION AND APPEARANCE

The monster begins to be educated to understand just how alien he is, and his refrain comes to be 'What was I?' (pp. 123, 124). He seems like a different species; he is hardier and more agile, but also deformed and loathsome – a 'blot on the earth' (p. 123). At times he wishes he had stayed in his natural state, and known nothing beyond the basic sensations. Knowledge comes to seem dangerous as it makes him aware of his difference. He learns that the only way out of the pain of consciousness is death, and in this way **foreshadows** the climax of the novel when he anticipates burning on his funeral pyre and, as ashes, finally returning to nature. On the other hand, the De Lacey household appears to be an egalitarian world, where there is an **atmosphere** of mutual concern, and difference can be accepted – they do, after all, embrace the Turkish Safie into their midst.

KEY QUOTATION: VOLUME TWO, CHAPTER V **A01**

'And what was I? Of my creation and creator I was absolutely ignorant, but I knew that I possessed no money, no friends, no kind of property' (p. 123).

Possible interpretations:

- Shows how the question of identity becomes central to the creature
- Demonstrates what the creature's education has taught him in terms of what is important: wealth and connections
- The language of 'creation and creator' anticipates his reading of *Paradise Lost* and his view of his self as an 'Adam'

REVISION FOCUS: TASK 2 **A02**

How far do you agree with the statement below?

- The monster's fate is determined by his appearance.

Try writing an opening paragraph for an essay based on this discussion point. Set out your arguments clearly.

CONTEXT **A02**

The **symbolic** names of the characters may be significant: Felix is happiness, Agatha goodness, and Safie is reminiscent of *sophia*, or wisdom.

CONTEXT **A04**

In Volney's *Ruins of Empire* (1791), a chapter on the 'Primitive State of Men' describes the earliest man as an orphan who has been deserted by the unknown powers that produced him and learns only by his senses.

VOLUME TWO, CHAPTER VI

SUMMARY

- The monster describes the history of the De Lacey family and of Safie.
- Safie's father, a Turkish merchant in Paris, was condemned to death for a minor crime. Felix planned the merchant's escape and fell in love with his daughter.
- Felix's plot was discovered. He, his father and sister, Agatha, were thrown in prison. On their release they took refuge in Germany and Safie eventually makes her way to their home.

ANALYSIS

SAFIE'S LETTERS

At the very centre of all the **narratives** in *Frankenstein* are the letters of Safie. Never actually reproduced, only summarised, they nevertheless bear a huge burden in proving the truth of the story. The monster hears the letters read aloud and, having acquired writing instruments, he copies them down. He will then offer these letters to Victor as 'proof' of his story, and Victor will in turn pass them on as 'proof' to Walton who will send them with his manuscript to Margaret Saville.

Why are these copied letters – actually letters exchanged between Safie and Felix – not reproduced? It could be partly that this is a way of ensuring no further narratives are **embedded** within. One could imagine, for example, if Safie's letters were reproduced, they might tell the story of her attendant, which, in turn might tell the story of another, and so on. The embedding could be endless, but Shelley instead decides to stop it here. And why should these unreproduced letters constitute any kind of proof or evidence of the truth of the story? Is there some kind of belief in the truth of language here? Or is it because this is the only narrative which is not written with the intention of persuasion? Critics have varied in their positions on this. What other possible explanations could you come up with?

CONTEXT `A04`

A comprehensive edition of the *Arabian Nights* was introduced to Europe at the beginning of the eighteenth century, inspiring an increased interest in things Oriental. Many **Romantic** poets wrote Orient-inspired works, including Coleridge's 'Kubla Khan' (1797). It also had an influence on the **Gothic**, with William Beckford's *Vathek* (1786) being the most notable example of Orientalist Gothic.

STUDY FOCUS: SAFIE'S STORY `A02`

The rather bizarre and improbable adventures related here provide Shelley with another opportunity to comment on the corruption of society and also establish that the De Laceys and Safie are, like the monster, aliens and exiles. Not that this will mean they will respond with sympathy to other aliens. The portrayal of Safie, who combines both masculine and feminine qualities, suggests Shelley does not consider the passivity and helplessness of Elizabeth as either positive or inevitable. Such critics as Joyce Zonana have, indeed, connected Safie to the work of Shelley's feminist mother, to Mary Wollstonecraft's *A Vindication of the Rights of Woman* (1792) in which, Zonana observes, 'references to the harem, to "Mahometanism" [become a figure for] an error she finds central to Western culture: the refusal to grant women full membership as rational beings in the human race' (Zonana, 'They Will Prove the Truth of My Tale', 1991, p. 173).

GLOSSARY

125	**Constantinople**	now called Istanbul
127	**Leghorn**	Livorno, Italy
128	**noisome**	foul-smelling
128	**asylum**	here used to suggest refuge

VOLUME TWO, CHAPTER VII

SUMMARY

- The monster discovers three books in the woods: *Paradise Lost*, a volume of Plutarch's *Lives* and Goethe's the *Sorrows of Werter*.

- He also discovers, in the clothing he took from the laboratory, Victor's journal from the months preceding his creation. He learns that Victor is repulsed by him and he curses Victor for abandoning him.

- He decides to approach the blind father when he is alone. All goes well until Felix, Safie and Agatha enter. Felix attacks him and the monster returns to his hovel.

ANALYSIS

THE EDUCATION CONTINUES

The reading of the three books, particularly *Paradise Lost*, plays a crucial role in the development of the monster's character and explains why he speaks as he does. The *Sorrows of Werter* expands his sensibilities and he applies the story to his own feelings and condition, intensifying his sense of alienation. If from Goethe he learns 'despondency and gloom' (p. 131), from Plutarch he learns 'high thoughts' (p. 131) and is raised beyond the misery of his own condition by stories of heroes. His admiration for virtue is consequently increased.

REJECTION

When the De Laceys reject the monster with horror, Shelley suggests how appearance is privileged in this society. Their domestic world survives only because of its insularity: that is, the De Laceys function only by excluding anything that appears as a potential threat to their security and are quite unable to cope with the intrusion of the monster into their world. They are no more capable than anyone else of seeing past his appearance and their treatment of him is what ultimately turns him towards evil.

STUDY FOCUS: THE VISUAL AND THE VERBAL (A02)

The monster's monstrosity is something emphatically visual from the start, and here it becomes clear that, in this society, only a blind man could accept him. Perhaps De Lacey's blindness represents the blindness of the reader. We too do not see the monster and so we are more concerned with what he says than with how he looks. When he is made visual through film, are we more likely to view him as monstrous? Consider the appearance of the monster as played by, for example, Charles Ogle in the Edison *Frankenstein* (1910), or the better-known version played by Boris Karloff in James Whale's Universal *Frankenstein* (1931).

GLOSSARY

131	**'The path of my departure was free'**	see Percy Bysshe Shelley, 'Mutability', 1.14
132	**Numa**	Numa Pompilius (fl. *c.* 700 BC), considered second of the seven kings of Ancient Rome
132	**Solon**	Greek statesman and legislator (*c.* 630–*c.* 560 BC)
132	**Lycurgus**	traditionally considered the lawgiver who founded the institutions of Sparta
132	**Romulus**	legendary founder of Rome
132	**Theseus**	legendary Greek hero

CHECK THE BOOK (A03)

Plutarch (*c.* AD 50–125) was a Greek biographer and moralist. His *Parallel Lives* illustrated the moral characters of his subjects through anecdote. *The Sorrows of Young Werther* (1774) by Johann Wolfgang von Goethe (1749–1832) is a semi-autobiographical novel about the life and ultimate suicide of a sensitive artist, hopelessly in love with a woman engaged to someone else.

CONTEXT (A03)

On page 134, there is a reference to 'Adam's supplication' – this refers to *Paradise Lost*, either 8.379 or 10.743–5, which Shelley used as the **epigraph** to *Frankenstein*. The monster sees his links with Adam, the first man, but also sees how they differ. Adam was happy and prosperous, cared for by his creator. Yet the monster is wretched and alone, thrown out of his Eden with no Eve to comfort him. Satan frequently seems a fitter comparison: when the monster observes the happiness of others, he is eaten up with envy.

VOLUME TWO, CHAPTER VIII

SUMMARY

- The De Laceys depart and the monster burns down their cottage. He starts out for Geneva, determined to seek help from Victor.
- On his journey he is shot by a man when he saves a girl from drowning.
- He falls asleep in the fields outside Geneva and is awoken by a young boy. He seizes the boy, planning to make him his companion.
- The child reveals he is William Frankenstein. The monster, wanting revenge, strangles him. He sees the miniature of Caroline and plants it on the sleeping Justine.
- The monster's narrative ends. He demands that Victor create a female companion.

ANALYSIS

REVENGE

Here is where the idea of the monster as the embodiment of revolutionary mob violence out of control is particularly clear. He becomes filled with feelings of revenge and hatred, and 'I did not strive to control them', he admits, 'but allowing myself to be borne away by the stream, I bent my mind towards injury and death' (p. 140). Notice how the weather reflects the monster's feelings, with the fierce winds producing a kind of insanity. In this respect the monster's relationship with nature is much like that of Victor's. Dancing in fury around the cottage with his fiery brand, the monster becomes a savage, irrational force. As soon as he becomes consumed by revenge, he begins to be truly monstrous. In this too he is just like Victor. Both monster and creator are driven and consumed by revenge; both become monstrous in their obsessions.

THE INNOCENTS

It is of some importance that the monster does not attack Victor; he takes his revenge by attacking family and friends. Most importantly, the victims of his attacks are all innocents: his point is surely that so was he. The monster's apparent malice in framing Justine is particularly disturbing, but he is nevertheless making an important point by enacting precisely the kind of arbitrary injustice to which he is subject when society repulses and demonises him purely on the basis of appearance. All this does not, of course, excuse his actions: he is not forced to make the choices he does.

STUDY FOCUS: NATURE AND NURTURE · A02

The question of nature and nurture is brought up by the monster himself, when he claims that he is made malicious by bad treatment. Is this true, or could one argue that he is intrinsically evil or unnatural because of the unnatural circumstances of his creation? Or is he originally neither good nor bad, but capable of being either?

GLOSSARY

138	**toils**	nets
138	**a hell within me**	*Paradise Lost*, 9.467: 'the hot hell that always in him burns'
141	**with the world before me**	an echo of the end of *Paradise Lost* where Adam and Eve leave Eden

CHECK THE BOOK · A01

Teratology is the term for the study of monsters (from the Greek *teras*, meaning monster or marvel). For a comprehensive history of monsters, see Stephen Asma's *On Monsters: An Unnatural History of Our Worst Fears* (2009).

CHECK THE FILM · A03

In James Whales's classic adaptation of *Frankenstein* (1931) the monster's actions are explained in terms of genetics: he was given a criminal's abnormal brain. The debate over nature or nurture is consequently made irrelevant.

EXTENDED COMMENTARY

VOLUME TWO, CHAPTER VIII PP. 144–5

This passage places us in the innermost **embedded narrative** of *Frankenstein*. The monster is reaching the conclusion of the story he tells Victor, whose own narrative serves to **frame** that of the monster. He recalls how, after being rejected by the De Laceys and shot by a villager whose child he saved from drowning, he finally determined on revenge for the injustice he has suffered. In focusing upon the monster's first murder, the moment when he becomes truly demonic, Shelley encourages us to consider how our personalities are formed and what forces can transform a man into a monster.

The passage begins as the monster is disturbed from sleep by the arrival of little William. He sees 'a beautiful child, who came running to the recess I had chosen, with all the sportiveness of infancy' (p. 144). The syntax could momentarily confuse us. It may initially seem as though the 'sportiveness of infancy' could refer to either William or the monster; it soon becomes clear, however, that both these 'children' have lost the wonder and innocence associated with the phrase. They have learned the lessons of society too well.

The monster wavers at the sight of William; his destructive impulses are momentarily buried again as he assumes that this little creature must be as yet 'unprejudiced' (p. 144) and therefore could be educated to be his companion and friend. The child, however, has already been socialised through the tales he has been told about 'ogres' and 'monsters' (p. 144). He has learned to abhor and fear anything that is alien and different. William displays just the same horror at the sight of the monster as all the others, even using one of Victor's favourite **epithets**: 'wretch' (p. 144). The scene may be said both to **parallel** and reverse the previous encounter with Felix. Like Felix, William simply assumes ugliness means threat and does not understand the real intentions of the monster. 'I do not intend to hurt you; listen to me' (p. 144), the monster says. Language has the power to hurt the monster, who is filled with despair by the epithets used by the child, but it has no power to check the overwhelming force of prejudice provoked by the visually alien. While Felix tries to protect his father from the threat, William invokes his father to protect him.

By this time, our sympathies may have been completely transferred to the monster; William seems like a nasty and spoilt little boy. It is precisely at this moment, however, that the monster becomes truly demonic. When William utters the name of Frankenstein, the monster's desire for revenge again surfaces and he strangles the child. He is now indeed satanic, his heart fills with 'hellish triumph' (p. 144), and he becomes increasingly so as this passage develops. He realises he can make Victor as desolate as he has made him. The monster displaces his aggression towards the father on to the son who invokes his name.

At the very moment the monster appears most horrific, he sees the miniature of Caroline. Women in this novel are notable primarily for their effect on others: Elizabeth has previously been called 'the living spirit of love to soften and attract' (p. 40). Caroline has a similar influence, even through the medium of her portrait. As he gazes on her loveliness, the monster finds that in spite of his malignity, 'it softened and attracted me'

CRITICAL VIEWPOINT **A03**

'Frankenstein's monster can be educated as a human being only if society is willing to accept him as such … Otherwise, he can be educated only to know the full extent of his exclusion, denied social identity by the very society he longs to join' (Anne McWhir, 'Teaching the Monster to Read', 1990, pp. 76–7).

CHECK THE FILM **A03**

Kenneth Branagh's *Mary Shelley's Frankenstein* (1994) establishes the idea of the **double** when the monster is shot and Frankenstein finds a wound corresponding to the monster's gunshot wound on his own body.

(p. 144). The response of little William, however, has settled one issue conclusively: no one, no matter how apparently innocent or gentle, will respond to the monster with kindness or affection. Remembering he is excluded by his ugliness from the delights women could bestow, the monster is again filled with rage and agony.

We know, although the monster does not, that Caroline is Victor's mother. Mothers in *Frankenstein*, as in most of Shelley's works, are notable mainly for their absence; they indicate a lack or a gap, something which is desired but prohibited. This is particularly true in the case of the monster, whose erotic gaze is fixed on the maternal figure that he, due to the circumstances of his birth, has been denied. This lack and this desire may be of particular significance if we consider the monster as Victor's **double**. Victor too has been denied his mother through death, and his fear of the sexuality which he sees as horrific is at least partly a fear of his incestuous desires. He longs for the mother, but also fears and hates her because he cannot possess her.

Soon after, the monster encounters Justine. The desire he has felt in gazing at the portrait is transferred to the woman he finds sleeping at his feet. While this scene has been described as a perverse fantasy of rape, there is far more tenderness than violence in the monster's language. Echoing Satan whispering seductively into the ear of the sleeping Eve in Milton's *Paradise Lost*, he whispers to Justine: 'Awake, fairest, thy lover is near' (p. 145). His attempt at seduction is halted, however, by the recollection that if Justine should awake she would denounce him as a murderer. All his satanic impulses now come to the fore: the 'fiend' (p. 144) stirs within him. The hostility he feels at being denied possession of the mother is transferred to this mother substitute, 'not indeed so beautiful as her whose portrait I held; but of an agreeable aspect' (p. 145). He decides to implicate Justine in the murder, condemning her because he cannot possess her.

As the monster notes, he is no longer an innocent. The treatment he has received from others has provided him with a good education in cruelty and injustice. 'The crime', he declares, 'had its source in her: be hers the punishment!' (p. 145). This is a strange claim and perhaps understandable only if, again, we see the monster as Victor's double, acting out Victor's aggression towards women, and, in particular, see the monster as an embodiment of Victor's destructive, and therefore horrific, sexuality, where the mother is desired but prohibited, and where the erotic is fused with the murderous.

This passage, then, lends itself to two quite different interpretations. If we read it from a sociological perspective, we might conclude that Shelley provides us with a critique of society and human injustice and an analysis of how our initially benevolent natures can be perverted through socialisation. If we read it from a psychological perspective, however, we might see Shelley as anticipating some of Freud's theories, and showing the monster/Victor to be acting out a displaced **Oedipal complex**. These two readings exist quite happily side by side, and Shelley seems to be suggesting that it is both the external forces that act upon us and the inner workings of the psyche that turn 'men' into 'monsters'.

CHECK THE BOOK **A03**

In an accessible discussion of *Frankenstein* and some of its film adaptations Abigail Bloom argues that film adaptations of nineteenth-century horror novels rarely show the close connections between the **protagonist** and the monstrous that are evident in the originals (*The Literary Monster on Film*, 2010).

VOLUME TWO, CHAPTER IX

SUMMARY

- Victor initially refuses the monster's request for a female companion.
- Victor is persuaded when the monster swears he will go into exile with his mate.
- Victor returns to Geneva and resolves to save his remaining family and friends by complying with the monster's request.

ANALYSIS

THE VEGETARIAN MONSTER

Vegetarianism is not a quality that we usually associate with monsters, but here the monster establishes his vegetarianism as a significant part of his identity: 'My food is not that of man; I do not destroy the lamb and the kid to glut my appetite' (p. 148). Consider this passage, in which the monster identifies his food, and the food that his proposed companion will eat. Why do you think this was included?

STUDY FOCUS: VISUAL AND VERBAL **A02**

Once again, there is an important distinction being made between the visual and the verbal. The chapter is full of references to the monster's ugliness. Victor calling the monster the 'filthy mass that moved and talked' (p. 149), for example, reduces it to a thing and denies any resemblance to the human. Similarly, Victor describes the monster's face as 'wrinkled into contortions too horrible for human eyes to behold' (p. 148). The monster has by now learned that he is condemned to isolation precisely because of his appearance: 'the human senses are insurmountable barriers to our union' (p. 148). Find other moments when the term 'human' is used in this chapter. Do you think there is consistency in the ways the term is used, or does any attempt to define the term clearly become problematic?

MONSTROUS AND HUMAN

Contrasting markedly with his creator's evident reluctance to settle his 'union' with Elizabeth, the monster's desire for companionship could be said to be one of his most human qualities. He desires to live with a female companion in a state of nature, eating acorns and berries and sleeping on dried leaves, and claims: 'The picture I present to you is peaceful and human' (p. 149). If this is the case, what assumptions are being made about the nature of the human?

REVISION FOCUS: TASK 3 **A01**

How far do you agree with the statement below?

- As with many **Gothic** texts, *Frankenstein* challenges set oppositions, in particular the opposition between the monstrous and the human.

Try writing an opening paragraph for an essay based on this discussion point. Set out your arguments clearly.

GLOSSARY

| 151 | **siroc** sirocco, a hot wind blowing from North Africa over the Mediterranean |

CONTEXT **A04**

Vegetarianism rose to prominence during the **Romantic** period, and Romantic vegetarians frequently interpreted the Fall in terms of meat eating – that is, the idea that Adam and Eve did not eat meat in Eden. Percy Bysshe Shelley wrote two articles advocating vegetarianism.

CRITICAL VIEWPOINT **A03**

Joanna Bourke's *What it Means to be Human* (Virago, 2011) starts from the position that the boundaries between the human and the non-human or animal are not fixed, but have constantly changed throughout history. Marking the boundaries between the human and the non-human is not a neutral exercise to set out a series of established facts, she argues; it is, rather, an exercise in power. Consider how this is applicable to *Frankenstein*.

VOLUME THREE, CHAPTER I

SUMMARY

- Victor, reluctant to begin work on the female companion, spends many weeks in Geneva. His father brings up the subject of his expected marriage to Elizabeth.
- Victor decides he must create the companion before marrying Elizabeth, and leaves for Britain.
- Clerval joins him on his travels and they arrive in London.

ANALYSIS

THAT DREADED UNION

'Alas!', exclaims Victor after his father asks him to marry without further delay, 'the idea of an immediate union with my Elizabeth was one of horror and dismay' (p. 157). He could not plan such an event, he explains, 'with this deadly weight yet hanging round my neck' (p. 157). Here he draws on an **image** from Coleridge's 'The Rime of the Ancient Mariner' (1798). The mariner, driven by guilt, must wear the bird he shoots around his neck; the albatross around the neck has become an idiomatic phrase to suggest a burden one carries.

But Victor's 'horror and dismay' seem rather excessive, and indeed much more connected to the idea of the 'immediate union with Elizabeth' than anything else. This forms a striking contrast with the monster's expression of desire for a mate with which the previous chapter concludes. Furthermore, notice how many times Victor uses the word 'union' when describing this exchange with his father. While Alphonse uses the more usual word – marriage – three times, Victor refers to the prospect of 'union' five times, and never uses the word marriage. Consider the different implications of those words 'marriage' and 'union'. On the one hand, 'union' might suggest a more formal social or legal contract; on the other hand, it is more indicative of a physical joining, of sexual union. It may well be that Victor, who prefers to do his creating on his own, fears a physical relationship with Elizabeth. We might recall, too, the dream of Elizabeth changing into the corpse of his mother in his arms. The idea that on one level it is Victor's sexuality that is monstrous will become clearer as the wedding night draws near.

CONTEXT A01

In earlier **Gothic** fictions, the castle is a key site, frequently a menacing place in which the heroine is imprisoned. With *Frankenstein*, however, the primary Gothic space changes to become Victor's horrific workshops. The 'ruined castles standing on the edges of precipices' (p. 160), that Victor and Clerval observe as they sail down the Rhine contain no threat and function only as part of the scenery.

STUDY FOCUS: HEALING NATURE A02

Compare Victor's response to nature here with those two earlier key moments you have already examined carefully: after the death of William (p. 76) and after the death of Justine (p. 94). Try to identify the features common to all these passages. Is there, for example, the repetition of particular words or phrases to suggest nature's healing powers? Is nature a maternal or benevolent figure?

GLOSSARY

155	**disquisition**	research
155	**philosopher**	scientist
156	**competent fortune**	sufficient money on which to live comfortably
159	**bourne**	destination, goal
161	**very poetry of nature**	ascribed by Shelley in the 1818 edition to Leigh Hunt's *The Story of Rimini* (1816), a narrative poem on the love affair of Paolo and Francesca
162	**Spanish Armada**	fleet sent by Philip II of Spain against England in 1588

VOLUME THREE, CHAPTER II

SUMMARY

- Victor and Clerval rest in London and then travel north to Scotland.
- Victor parts from Clerval and goes to the remotest of the Orkney Islands where he begins to work on making the female companion.

ANALYSIS

THE ORKNEY ISLANDS

The Orkney Islands offer an appropriately remote setting for the creation of the female companion. It may be significant that Victor creates the male in the university town of Ingolstadt, connected to intellectual pursuits, whereas for the female he leases a squalid hut on a barren island little more than a rock: a 'desolate and appalling landscape' (pp. 168–9). This, he says, is 'a place fitted for such a work' (p. 168). Compare Victor's present reluctance for his 'labours' – and notice the number of times this word recurs (pp. 168–9) – with his enthusiasm for his previous 'midnight labours' (p. 55). This time he is sickened by what he does; perhaps his view of the landscape is a reflection of his state of mind. He has significantly described himself during his travels with Clerval in terms of a devastated nature, 'a blasted tree' (p. 165).

CHECK THE BOOK **A03**

Mary Shelley wrote travelogues as well as fiction. *History of a Six Weeks' Tour* (1817) was written with Percy Shelley and based on their elopement to the Continent in 1814. *Rambles in Germany and Italy* (1844) concerns her recollections of later travels with her son and his friends in search of improved health.

STUDY FOCUS: ROMANTIC VERSUS GOTHIC   **A01**

Many of Victor's descriptions of the landscape reflect the ideals of **Romanticism**. These include the trip down the Rhine with Clerval (pp. 160–2) and Victor's journey through the valley of Chamounix (pp. 97–8). Compare these previous descriptions of the landscape with the far more Gothic landscape of the Orkneys in this chapter (pp. 168–9). There is nothing uplifting or restorative here. Rather, there is a sense of dread and entrapment, combined with a brooding paranoia and the threat of violence. Landscape combines with weather to produce a raw and primitive world, and in this way can be compared with the desolate and stormy moors of Emily Brontë's *Wuthering Heights*.

GLOSSARY

165	**Charles I**	Charles I (1600–49) was executed after his defeat in the Civil War
165	**Falkland**	Lucius Carey, Viscount Falkland (1610–43), Secretary of State under Charles I
165	**Goring**	George, Baron Goring (1608–57), Royalist general
165	**Isis**	name given to the River Thames at Oxford
165	**verdure**	fresh greenness
165	**Hampden**	John Hampden (1594–1643), Parliamentarian, killed at Chalgrove Field
166	**wondrous cave**	probably High Tor Grotto near Matlock

CRITICAL VIEWPOINT **A03**

In *Frankenstein*, the healing Romantic landscapes seem to act upon the observer; the Gothic landscapes more frequently suggest that the observer is acting upon them: that is, the landscape becomes a reflection of an internal state of mind. See, for example, the paranoia and guilt in Victor's description of himself as following Henry like his shadow: 'I felt as if I had committed some great crime, the consciousness of which haunted me' (p. 167).

VOLUME THREE, CHAPTER III

SUMMARY

- Victor begins to consider further the potentially disastrous effects of creating a mate for the monster.
- The monster appears at the window and Victor tears the new creation apart before his eyes. The monster promises to be with Victor on his wedding night.
- Victor, planning to join Clerval for the trip home, first sets off in a boat to throw the remains of the female into the sea. He gets lost and is washed ashore in Ireland where he is immediately arrested for murder.

ANALYSIS

MONSTERS AND MOONLIGHT

This is the second of the three occasions when Victor sees the monster by moonlight. The first time follows Victor's dream of Elizabeth turning into the corpse of his dead mother in his arms; he wakes with horror from his sleep and sees the monster with a grin wrinkling his cheeks and stretching out his hand (p. 59). When Victor sees the monster by moonlight for the second time here, there is again a 'ghastly grin' (p. 171), and, once again, Victor seems to misinterpret the monster's intentions. We may assume the monster's grin is a sign of his delight, but Victor interprets what he sees as an expression of 'malice and treachery' (p. 171). While he does not appear very discerning, the misinterpretation is probably explained by his previous thoughts. He has wanted an excuse to stop making the female, and the idea that the monster is treacherous and will not, as he has sworn, 'quit the neighbourhood of man' (p. 170) serves to justify tearing the mate apart.

When the monster returns, he threatens Victor, 'I shall be with you on your wedding-night' (p. 173), and Victor – again rather obtusely – assumes this means that is the moment when the monster will try to kill him. Given that Victor has just destroyed the monster's prospective mate, one might think it rather obvious that the monster's threat is directed at Elizabeth and, indeed, the murder of Elizabeth will be the third moment when the monster will be seen by moonlight.

MOONLIGHT AS METAPHOR

In terms of **Gothic** horror, the moon might immediately bring to mind the werewolf, and this is the clearest example of how the moon is connected to change, to the emergence of another self, more bestial, more primitive perhaps. This may be linked to the idea of Victor and the monster as **doubles**: that is, when the moon reveals the monster, it is also illuminating something within Victor.

CONTEXT **A04**

In her 1831 Introduction, Shelley claims that her inspiration for *Frankenstein* came during a waking dream as the moon shone through her window (p. 9). John Polidori's diary account of events suggests this happened on 16 June 1816. In 2011 a Texan astronomer, Donald Olson, investigated weather records for June 1816 in the area of the Villa Diodati. On the basis of astronomical data he confirmed that a bright gibbous (more than half illuminated) moon would indeed have shone right into Shelley's bedroom window just before 2.00 am on 16 June 1816.

VOLUME THREE, CHAPTER IV

SUMMARY

- Victor is taken before the magistrate and begins to suspect the murdered man is Clerval. His suspicions are confirmed when he is taken to see the corpse.

- Victor collapses and spends two months in a fever. In his delirium he confesses to the murders of William, Justine and Clerval.

- Alphonse Frankenstein comes to Ireland. Victor is eventually acquitted.

ANALYSIS

THE LANGUAGE OF PERSECUTION

Victor's account of his time in prison is, like the monster's account of his experiences with society, a **narrative** of persecution: 'I am', he exclaims, 'the most miserable of mortals. Persecuted and tortured as I am and have been, can death be any evil to me?' (p. 183). Both Victor and his monster consistently represent themselves as victims, and there are times when it seems close to becoming a competition to see who can claim to suffer the most. Remember, for example, Victor's comment on the night before Justine's execution: the poor victim, he exclaims, 'felt not, as I did, such deep and bitter agony' (p. 89). And look out for the monster's later claim as he hangs over Victor's corpse: 'Blasted as thou wert, my agony was still superior to thine' (p. 225). We may well feel inclined to sympathise with Walton when he berates the monster for having come to 'whine' (p. 223) over desolation for which he must take some responsibility.

Why do you think Shelley has both Victor and the monster constantly represent themselves using the **rhetoric** of the victim? Is it perhaps evidence that both become completely obsessed and self-absorbed? On one level this is part of Shelley's critique of **Romanticism**. The language of persecution is often found within Romantic poetry, suggesting the sensitive soul buffeted by the unfeeling world or even by fate itself.

> **CONTEXT** A03
>
> Percy Bysshe Shelley has one particularly notorious example of how the Romantics exploit victim rhetoric in his 'Ode to the West Wind'. Appropriating Christian **imagery** of the crucifixion, he somewhat dramatically exclaims: 'I fall upon the thorns of life, I bleed' (line 54).

STUDY FOCUS: THE MONSTER WITHIN VICTOR A02

Metaphorically, in this chapter the boundary between Victor and his monster is completely broken down. This is initially suggested by the way Victor confesses fault for the murders ('Have my murderous machinations...', p. 181). Literally, he may mean these murders are the result of him creating the monster, but the language suggests something much more than this. And in the nightmare that closes the chapter the monster even appears to be part of his body: 'I felt the fiend's grasp *in* my neck; and could not free myself from it; groans and cries rang in my ears' (p. 188, emphasis added). Each part of this sentence is worth pausing over. Why, for example is it 'in my neck' and not 'on my neck'? What about the **ambiguity** in the second phrase? And finally, why does he hear the groans and cries of the victims in his ears? In the chapters that follow, you should be able to find even more examples of the way the boundaries between Victor and his monster break down.

> **CRITICAL VIEWPOINT** A03
>
> 'Despite his commitment to science, Frankenstein fails to realize what Mary Shelley realizes in her introduction: in the modern world, human beings are not spoken to in dreams; they are speaking to themselves. The dream does not invade the dreamer; it is invented by the dreamer' (Ronald Thomas, *Dreams of Authority*, 1990, p. 90).

GLOSSARY

187	*maladie du pays*	(French) homesickness
187	**Havre-de-Grâce**	original name of the French port of Le Havre

VOLUME THREE, CHAPTER V

SUMMARY

- Victor receives a letter from Elizabeth asking if he regrets his commitment to marry her. He reassures her, returns to Geneva, and they are married.
- They start the journey to Lake Como for their honeymoon.

ANALYSIS

'I WILL BE WITH YOU ON YOUR WEDDING NIGHT...'

Elizabeth's letter reminds Victor of their intended union, and this revives the memory of the monster's threat: 'I will be with you on your wedding night', a phrase he italicises and repeats, with slight variation, three times in the chapter. Victor continues to interpret this as meaning that is the night on which the monster will attempt to kill him, although it is clear to the reader that the threat is to Elizabeth. Is it the letter or the revived memory of the threat that persuades him, after so many years, to marry Elizabeth?

When Victor finally makes reference to what the monster really means, he completely rejects any possibility that he could have known beforehand. If he had suspected what might be the monster's 'hellish intention' (p. 195), he declares, he would never have married Elizabeth. 'But, as if possessed of magic powers, the monster had blinded me to his real intentions' (p. 195). 'Magic powers' certainly a strange phrase for someone who professes to be a scientist. Victor frequently draws on the language of the supernatural to describe what we understand only as a psychological condition. He does not see that there are no 'magic powers' at work: these are only symptoms of his disordered mind.

GRADE BOOSTER A02

Examiners will be impressed if you demonstrate close attention to the language, particularly, as in Victor's use of the term 'magic powers', when dialogue contributes to characterisation.

STUDY FOCUS: NARRATIVE LINKS A02

The moment in which Victor decides to marry Elizabeth (p. 193) links to a previous scene in which apparent professions of love combine with an underlying impetus towards violence (pp. 144–5). The monster has just burned down the De Lacey cottage in fury and come to Geneva seeking Victor; he meets and murders William and plants the portrait of Caroline on Justine. Consider and compare these key moments, looking in particular at the effects of the portrait of Caroline compared with the effects of the letter of Elizabeth; the seductive whispering in the ear at each moment; the decision to set up Justine for the murder and the decision to marry Elizabeth. As the monster's actions lead to the death of Justine, Victor's actions lead to the death of Elizabeth.

GLOSSARY

191	**sea of ice** the glacier Mer de Glace
195	**nicer** more perceptive
195	**decorations** used in archaic sense to refer to scenery on stage
196	**artifice** trickery
196	**Evian** resort on Lake Geneva

VOLUME THREE, CHAPTER VI

SUMMARY

- As night falls, a storm arises and Victor is increasingly agitated. He sends Elizabeth to their room and goes to see if he can discover the location of the monster.
- Elizabeth is murdered by the monster. Victor returns to Geneva. His father, heartbroken, dies.
- Victor spends some time in a mental asylum and on his release determines on revenge. He tells the story to a magistrate who will not take any action.

ANALYSIS

LIVING THE DREAM

As any viewer of contemporary horror films knows, Victor is asking for trouble in leaving Elizabeth alone in the night. When he recovers from his faint and finds Elizabeth's body, he momentarily supposes she might be asleep; he rushes towards her and 'embraced her with ardour; but the deadly languor and coldness of the limbs told me, that what I now held in my arms had ceased to be the Elizabeth whom I had loved and cherished' (p. 199). The dream of Elizabeth turning into the corpse of the dead mother in his arms as he kisses her (p. 59) is now enacted, the veiled face serving to draw attention to the possibility that here will be the dead mother of the dream, with all its incestuous implications.

We could argue that killing Elizabeth is, on a more abstract level, killing the mother. The language used to describe the subsequent appearance of the monster at the window by moonlight, pointing to the corpse of Elizabeth with a grin wrinkling his face, echoes the language used to describe that dreary night when he was created. Death and birth are again linked, taking us back to the nightmare that followed the creation and suggesting the fears that produced that nightmare have now been actualised.

STUDY FOCUS: WEATHER FORECASTS **A02**

By now, the reader has come to expect that changes in the weather will be followed by the arrival of the monster. At the start of this chapter, the change is particularly sudden. Victor and Elizabeth arrive at Evian, where they will spend their wedding night. They walk on the shore, retire to the inn, and continue to contemplate the mountains, now obscure black outlines. Within one paragraph, night falls and the weather changes: the wind rises 'with great violence', the waters of the lake become rough, and there is a 'heavy storm of rain' (p. 198).

Weather is frequently a trigger for **pathetic fallacy**, the projection of human emotions onto phenomena in the natural world, and here we have an excellent example of this. As the weather changes, suggesting outer turbulence reflects inner, Victor becomes agitated and night falls. Consider the **ambiguity** of his comforting words to Elizabeth: 'peace, peace, my love … this night, and all will be safe: but this night is dreadful, very dreadful' (p. 198). They are not the words Elizabeth might have expected on her wedding night.

GLOSSARY

199	**bier**	where a corpse is laid before burial
201	*acme*	culmination or high point

CRITICAL VIEWPOINT A03

'Apart from the odd storm at sea, weather was given scant attention in prose fiction until the late eighteenth century. In the nineteenth century, novelists always seem to be talking about it. This was the consequence partly of the heightened appreciation of Nature engendered by **Romantic** poetry and painting, partly of a growing literary interest in the individual self, in states of feeling that affect and are affected by our perceptions of the external world' (David Lodge, *The Art of Fiction*, 1993, p. 85).

CONTEXT A04

Henry Fuseli's *The Nightmare* (1781) may well have inspired the scene of Elizabeth's death. The painting depicts a woman stretched across a bed. An incubus, or male demon, crouches on her torso and a horse, the 'nightmare', with gleaming eyes and teeth bared, peers through the curtain. The painting suggests both terror and a vague sense of oppression.

VOLUME THREE, CHAPTER VII

SUMMARY

CHECK THE BOOK **A03**

For a discussion of film versions of the novel, see Steven Earl Forry, *Hideous Progenies: Dramatizations of 'Frankenstein' from Mary Shelley to the Present* (University of Pennsylvania Press, 1990).

- Victor concludes his story with an account of his determination on revenge and his pursuit of the monster.
- He asks Walton to continue his quest to find and kill the monster if he should die.
- Walton takes over the story again in letters to Margaret. It looks as though the ship may be destroyed by ice floes, and Victor fears mutiny.
- The sailors demand to return home; Victor attempts to raise their courage, but ultimately Walton must promise to turn back when the ice permits it.
- Victor dies and Walton later finds the monster in the cabin, bending over Victor and full of remorse.
- The monster tells Walton of the anguish he suffered, and then, with the intention of destroying himself, he springs from the cabin window and is gone.

ANALYSIS

VICTOR'S MADNESS

As Victor begins to describe his pursuit of the monster over Europe, Russia and eventually into the Arctic, it becomes increasingly clear that his mind is unhinged. (We remember he was locked up in a dungeon in an asylum in the previous chapter.) When Victor goes to the cemetery, he thinks the spirits of the departed hover around. But this remains a secular world, and the idea of spirits emphasises Victor's delusions. As Victor curses and becomes possessed by rage, he hears in response only the 'fiendish laugh' (p. 206) of the monster. Throughout his journey, what Victor considers to be the actions of the good spirits of the departed – the food left for him, for example – are of course only the actions of the monster.

CHECK THE FILM **A03**

In the first *Frankenstein* film, a fifteen-minute silent film made by the Edison Film Company in 1910, **doubling** is suggested through a mirror. In the final scene, the monster sees his own reflection; Frankenstein enters the room, the monster's reflection fades and is replaced by that of Frankenstein.

STUDY FOCUS: THE MERGING OF VICTOR AND THE MONSTER **A02**

All three **narratives** come together in this final chapter, and Victor and his monster become almost indistinguishable. Both are full of fury and bent on revenge; both consider themselves the most miserable. There is even a moment when Walton's description of Victor suggests the duality of his being, the emergence of the monster within. The tranquil voice and fine and lovely eyes disappear and, 'like a volcano bursting forth, his face would suddenly change to an expression of the wildest rage' (p. 212). It is a moment of transformation that looks forward to Jekyll becoming Hyde.

To demonstrate further how close Victor and the monster have become, try to decide who is speaking here at this earlier moment in the text: 'I wandered like an evil spirit, for I had committed deeds of mischief beyond description horrible'. What about: 'I had begun life with benevolent intentions … Now all was blasted'. Is this Victor speaking, or the monster? Can you be absolutely sure? Who hates and who suffers the most? You will find the answer on page 93 of the novel.

FIRE AND ICE

In 'Fire and Ice in *Frankenstein*' (1979), Andrew Griffin points out that while fire is associated with life, 'vital fire or fiery life', ice is what negates fire: it blights and kills; it is repression and death (pp. 49–50). The two extremes are frequently brought together in *Frankenstein*, from Walton's dream of eternal sunshine at the North Pole to Victor's dream of the vital fire or spark that will animate dead matter, and finally, in the last chapter, to the monster's plan to seek the furthest northern extremity and there light his funeral pyre and 'consume to ashes' his 'miserable frame' (p. 224). There is a reversal of the extremes of creation here: rather than cold limbs being brought together into a whole and infused with the fire of life, fire will return the frame to ashes, and his 'burning miseries' will be made visible and consumed by the 'torturing flames' (p. 225).

GOTHIC ENDINGS

In the eighteenth-century **Gothic** fictions of such writers as Ann Radcliffe, the villains are defeated and the heroine, after her extensive adventures, is finally reinstated within middle-class society through her marriage. This is the kind of ending **parodied** by Jane Austen in *Northanger Abbey* (1818) when she concludes that readers 'will see in the tell-tale compression of the pages before them, that we are all hastening together to perfect felicity'.

There is no sense of 'perfect felicity' in *Frankenstein*. All quests end in failure and the body count is remarkably high. Furthermore, the ending is marked by **ambiguity**. It is an example of an 'open ending' (David Lodge, *The Art of Fiction*, 1993, p. 224), leaving the sense of an open future. What will happen to Walton? Does the monster actually kill himself? We cannot say with any certainty since all that is in the future, beyond the boundaries of the text and therefore, like the monster itself, 'lost in darkness and distance' (p. 225).

GLOSSARY

206	**the furies possessed me**	the furies were Graeco-Roman goddesses of vengeance, sent to punish men for their crimes; they were particularly concerned with those who neglected family duties
209	**The Greeks wept for joy**	Xenophon (431–*c*. 350 BC) records this in Anabasis, when he describes leading the Greek soldiers out of Asia in 400 BC
214	**projectors**	promoters of speculative schemes
219	**a composing draught**	a sedative
222	**Evil thenceforth became my good**	*Paradise Lost*, 4.108–10: 'Evil, be thou my good'

KEY QUOTATION: VOLUME THREE, CHAPTER VII A01

Victor describes himself to Walton: 'like the archangel who aspired to omnipotence, I am chained in an eternal hell' (p. 214).

Possible interpretations:

- Victor links himself to Milton's Satan, as does the monster, thereby bringing the two closer together
- Continues the motif of the **Romantic** satanic hero
- Suggests that hell is something internal

REVISION FOCUS: TASK 4 A04

How far do you agree with the statement below?

- Victor's downfall is the result of his search for knowledge.

Try writing an opening paragraph for an essay based on this discussion point. Set out your arguments clearly.

CRITICAL VIEWPOINT A02

Find all the language relating to fire and ice in this final chapter. How do you think it functions? Is there a sense of reconciliation of extremes? Or is the monster's projected lonely death an assertion of his selfhood, an assertion of his humanity?

GRADE BOOSTER A01

Novelists may have reasons for leaving endings 'open', but for an essay you need a strong conclusion that will refer back to your central argument, tie your ideas together and leave an impression on your reader. You might end with a quotation, evoke a vivid **image** (think how effective the alliteration is in Shelley's 'darkness and distance'), ask a provocative question, or just suggest the results or consequences of your conclusion. But avoid a simple repetition of what you have already said, and avoid the boring and mechanical 'In conclusion …'.

CHARACTERS

VICTOR FRANKENSTEIN

WHO IS VICTOR FRANKENSTEIN?

- Victor is the son of Alphonse and Caroline; brother of Ernest and William; adoptive brother and later husband to Elizabeth and the childhood friend of Henry Clerval.
- He creates a giant being but abandons him.
- The monster begins to avenge himself on Victor's family, and Victor is persuaded to make him a female companion, which he ultimately rips to pieces.
- Clerval and Elizabeth are murdered and Victor follows the monster into the Arctic where he meets Walton. He dies on board Walton's ship.

ALIENATION

Like the monster, Victor is an isolated individual; his alienation, however, is self-imposed. While the monster longs for the companionship and affection he is denied, Victor avoids and rejects the family and friends who love him. He claims this is necessary in order to pursue his quest for the secret of life. There are many suggestions in the text, however, that Victor is rebelling against all human ties, against those human relationships that bind one to a family or community, against familial and sexual love – all relationships that might interfere with the pursuit of his own needs and desires.

CONTEXT A04

Prometheus was a popular figure with the Romantic poets, who emphasised his role as the suffering champion of humankind and the archetypal rebel hero.

STUDY FOCUS: A MODERN PROMETHEUS A03

Victor, as the subtitle of the novel suggests, is a searcher after forbidden knowledge, one of those Promethean overreachers who refuse to accept limitations and are subsequently punished. He is, however, more specifically a 'modern' Prometheus. This is an entirely secular world – there are no gods for this Prometheus to steal fire from – and all is achieved through science. The analogy with Prometheus raises a number of questions about Victor. Is he really driven by a desire to help humankind or is he driven by a desire for personal glory? Is his real crime the creation of a being, or is it his failure to take responsibility for what he creates?

CRITICAL VIEWPOINT A03

Chris Baldick compares Victor's story with that of Marlowe's Doctor Faustus: both men make a dangerous pact with forces they do not really understand. But the world of *Frankenstein* is an entirely secular world – no gods, no demons. While Faust's damnation is brought about by Mephistopheles, Baldick argues, 'Victor Frankenstein has no serious tempter other than himself' (Chris Baldick, *In Frankenstein's Shadow*, 1990, p. 42).

ROMANTICISM

Contemporary critics often consider that, through Victor, Shelley criticises the egocentric and antisocial tendencies of **Romanticism**. She pushes the Romantic figure of the isolated creative imagination to its extremes and demonstrates the dangers associated with solitude and introversion. Victor resembles the Romantic artist in the way he repeatedly claims to suffer for his aspirations. Indeed, he and the monster vie with each other to claim the most suffering.

KEY QUOTATIONS: VICTOR A01

- Victor's ambition: 'A new species would bless me as its creator and source' (p. 55).
- On his work: 'I pursued nature to her hiding-places. Who shall conceive the horrors of my secret toil …?' (p. 55).
- Last words to Walton: 'Seek happiness in tranquillity, and avoid ambition … why do I say this? I have myself been blasted in these hopes, yet another may succeed' (p. 220).

The Monster

Who is the Monster?

- He is created and then abandoned by Frankenstein. Spurned and attacked by all, he begins to avenge himself on Frankenstein by murdering William and framing Justine.
- He meets Victor and demands a mate. In revenge for Victor's destruction of his companion the monster kills first Clerval and then Elizabeth.
- The monster leads Victor across Europe and into the Arctic. When Victor dies, he appears to mourn him and then disappears.

The Monster's Education

In spite of his unnatural origins, the monster can initially be seen as a new Adam or a **noble savage**: he claims to be benevolent, innocent and free from prejudice. As his education continues, and he moves from learning about nature to culture, he learns about injustice in society. He also learns about emotions and comes to desire love and companion-ship, but he is rejected and denied these because of his appearance. Peter Brooks suggests that the story of the monster's education 'is a classic study of right natural instinct perverted and turned evil by the social milieu' (see, 'Godlike Science/Unhallowed Arts', 1979, p. 215).

The character of Caliban in Shakespeare's *The Tempest* may well have influenced Shelley. Prospero berates Caliban for his behaviour and reminds Caliban how he was taught and educated. Caliban says, 'You taught me language, and my profit on't/ Is I know how to curse. The red plague rid you/ For learning me your language!' It is arguable whether this is the same or a converse situation to the monster's – the classic nature versus nurture argument.

CRITICAL VIEWPOINT A03

David Lodge argues that in a novel 'names are never neutral. They always signify, if it is only ordinariness' (*The Art of Fiction*, 1993, p. 37). In terms of the monster's search for identity, then, it must also signify that Shelley does not give him a name at all.

Study Focus: The Monster Speaks · A02

The monster, perhaps unsurprisingly given his reading material (*Paradise Lost*, a volume of Plutarch's *Lives* and the *Sorrows of Werter*), is eloquent, a master of **rhetoric**. He believes that if he acquires language he will convince the De Lacey family to overlook his appearance and accept him. He masters language, but does that language in any way save him? What does he learn from what he reads and hears? It could be argued that, instead of allowing him entrance into society, his mastery of language serves only to make him more fully aware of his unique origin and alien nature. In this respect, perhaps his education is part of what makes him miserable.

CHECK THE FILM A03

Whereas Shelley's monster not only speaks but also speaks eloquently, the majority of film adaptations, beginning with James Whale's *Frankenstein* (1931), make the monster mute. This of course means he cannot tell his side of the story. It could be argued that this reduces the complexity of the monster and the novel as a whole.

The Double

The monster convinces Victor that he should have a companion, arguing that he is malicious because he is miserable (p. 147). He turns on Victor's family and friends because they represent to Victor what Victor has denied to him: the comforts of domestic affection. But in so far as the monster is Victor's **double**, the expression of a split within his psyche, the monster is murdering all those whom Victor has already attempted to cut off in his obsessive search for the secret of life. In this respect, he may represent Victor's own aggressive instincts, his fears of the family and of women (see **Themes**).

Key Quotations: The Monster · A01

- The question posed by the monster's education: 'What was I?' (pp. 123, 124).
- The monster after being rejected by the De Laceys: 'I, like the arch fiend, bore a hell within me' (p. 138).

ROBERT WALTON

WHO IS ROBERT WALTON?

- Walton is an explorer and ship's captain on an Arctic expedition in search of the Northwest Passage to the Pacific Ocean.
- He rescues Victor, who tells him the **narrative** of his life and the monster's narrative.
- Walton writes down these narratives and plans to send the manuscript to his sister, Margaret Saville, in England.

ANOTHER VICTOR?

In some respects, Walton may be seen as a **double** for Victor Frankenstein. He rebels against his father's dying instruction that he should not go to sea in much the same way as Victor rebels against Alphonse Frankenstein's dismissal of his readings in alchemy: each son subsequently pursues the forbidden. As Victor seeks to penetrate the secrets of nature, Walton seeks to find and penetrate the Northwest Passage: human geography is replaced by natural geography. Like Victor, Walton is obsessed by his quest, and, like Victor, he leaves the placid domestic world embodied by his sister Margaret for the outside world of action and achievement, showing a reckless disregard for human consequences.

OR NOT?

There are also some differences between the two men. In his search for knowledge, while equally obsessive, Walton is not quite as isolated as Victor, whose secret activities keep him hidden and alone. Walton must rely on his crew to fulfil his ambitions. When they insist on returning home, he is saved from becoming like Victor and destroying all through his 'mad schemes' (p. 215). Not, of course, that Walton appreciates being thus 'saved' in the least. He is bitter until the end about what he sees as his crew's 'cowardice and indecision' (p. 218).

STUDY FOCUS: FRIENDSHIP A02

While, like Victor, Walton leaves behind family and friends in pursuit of glory, he frequently complains of loneliness to his sister: 'I have no friend' (p. 18). There is no one amongst his crew, he suggests, who is cultivated enough to satisfy his needs. But what does 'friendship' really seem to involve in *Frankenstein*? On meeting Victor, Walton almost immediately begins to 'love him as a brother' (p. 28), to see him as 'the brother of my heart' (p. 28). The repeated use of this family term is surely of some importance given that Walton is actually escaping from the domestic world.

Victor is his 'brother' in the sense that Walton recognises himself in Victor. Once we understand this, his praise of Victor, his claim that Victor must have been a 'glorious creature' (p. 214) in his prime, becomes much more understandable. This is one more example of Walton's narcissistic self-regard, a characteristic he shares with Victor. Friendship is indeed idealised in *Frankenstein*, but like most other things it is perverted through egotism: Walton is seeking not so much a friend as someone just like himself.

KEY QUOTATIONS: ROBERT WALTON A01

- Walton on glory: 'My life might have been passed in ease and luxury; but I preferred glory to every enticement that wealth placed in my path' (p. 17).
- On his ambition to find the Northwest Passage: 'you cannot contest the inestimable benefit which I shall confer on all mankind to the last generation' (p. 16).
- Walton on Victor: 'What a glorious monster must he have been in the days of his prosperity, when he is thus noble and godlike in ruin!' (p. 214).

CHECK THE FILM A03

Most film adaptations of *Frankenstein* – Kenneth Branagh's *Mary Shelley's Frankenstein* (1994) being one notable exception – dispense with the character of Robert Walton and with the whole idea of a **frame narrative**. Since one of Walton's functions is to emphasise and help reveal Victor's faults, it could be argued that much is lost by this omission.

CRITICAL VIEWPOINT A03

'While the main theme of the novel is the monstrous consequences of egotism, the counter-theme is the virtue of friendship. For, as Frankenstein's crime is seen as a sin against humankind more than against the heavens, it is through human sympathy, rather than divine grace, that it might have been avoided or redeemed' (Robert Kiely, *The Romantic Novel in England*, 1972, pp. 166–7).

ALPHONSE AND CAROLINE FRANKENSTEIN

WHO ARE ALPHONSE AND CAROLINE FRANKENSTEIN?

- Alphonse and Caroline are the parents of Victor, Ernest and William, and the adopted parents of Elizabeth.
- Caroline Beaufort looks after her father until his death; Alphonse Frankenstein then saves her from poverty and marries her.
- Caroline contracts scarlet fever when nursing Elizabeth and dies. Alphonse dies after hearing of the death of Elizabeth.

AN IDEAL OF FEMININITY

Caroline serves primarily to establish an ideal of femininity that will then be reproduced in other female characters. Before her marriage she has a certain hardiness and independence. Her father's pride makes him willing to remain idle and suffer, and let his daughter suffer, while he waits for employment suitable to his position. Once he is ill, however, Caroline does 'plain work' (p. 34) to support him. From the start, Caroline's hardiness is mixed in with the tendency towards self-sacrifice. While there may be deep love between Caroline and Alphonse, her husband's protective care means she loses some independence. She participates in the larger world only as 'guardian angel to the afflicted' (p. 36). The rest of her time is devoted to her family. In the ultimate act of self-denial, she dies saving Elizabeth.

DOMESTIC BLISS

Alphonse is, initially at least, a public figure of some importance. He retires from the world once he becomes a husband and father, emphasising the opposition between the public sphere of action and the private sphere of the domestic affections (see **Themes**). Unlike Victor, with his rejection of his responsibilities towards his 'children', Alphonse and Caroline are very aware of their duties towards their son. They are indulgent but firm parents, guiding with a 'silken cord' (p. 35), but Victor later sees his childhood life as 'remarkably secluded and domestic' (p. 46) and he is consequently happy to leave this hot-house of family affection where all are engaged in 'endeavouring to bestow mutual pleasure' (p. 46).

CRITICAL VIEWPOINT A02

Two portraits of Caroline are mentioned in the text: the miniature worn by William and the painting of her kneeling by the coffin of her dead father. But perhaps we could say the text is full of reproductions of Caroline, with the other female characters just more copies, part of an extensive series of reproductions of the devoted daughter/wife/mother.

STUDY FOCUS: GOTHIC FATHERS A02

Fatherhood in **Gothic** writing, as Dale Townshend notes, is seldom 'naturally or biologically derived'; rather, it is 'based upon a complex process of metaphorical substitution' (Townshend, *The Orders of Gothic*, 2007, p. 98). While this may be most clearly shown in *Frankenstein* through the creation of the monster, it is also evident in the relationship of Caroline and Alphonse. The painting commissioned by Alphonse in which Caroline is immortalised 'in an agony of despair, kneeling by the coffin of her dead father' (p. 79) reminds us that Alphonse was an intimate friend of Beaufort and was attracted to Caroline by her devotion to her father. Indeed, Alphonse is old enough to be Caroline's father, and he assumes the role of father in taking over as protector.

KEY QUOTATIONS: ALPHONSE AND CAROLINE FRANKENSTEIN A01

- Alphonse as protector: 'He strove to shelter her, as a fair exotic is sheltered by the gardener' (p. 35).
- Caroline is: 'guardian angel to the afflicted' (p. 36).
- Their sense of duty as parents: 'this deep consciousness of what they owed towards the being to which they had given life' (p. 35).

ELIZABETH LAVENZA AND JUSTINE MORITZ

WHO IS ELIZABETH LAVENZA?

- Elizabeth is an orphan of noble origins adopted by the Frankenstein family. Caroline intends that Victor should marry her.
- Victor and Elizabeth marry after Clerval's death. The monster murders Elizabeth on their wedding night.

ELIZABETH AND THE IDEAL WOMAN

'Fairer than a garden rose among dark-leaved brambles' (p. 36), Elizabeth is initially singled out for her beauty. Caroline Frankenstein moulds her into the 'ideal' woman, a role she avidly embraces. Like the monster, Elizabeth is set apart, and viewed as a being of a 'distinct species' (p. 36). Religious **imagery** colours descriptions of the 'heaven-sent' (p. 36) Elizabeth, whose name means 'gift of God'. With her 'celestial eyes' and 'saintly soul' (p. 39), she is highly spiritualised, and, unlike later voluptuous screen Elizabeths, less a creature of flesh and blood than a 'living spirit of love' (p. 40). She is generally characterised in terms of her effects on others. Her ability to 'soften and attract' (p. 40) is seen as woman's most treasured gift. She is the opposite of the egotistical Victor. Self-effacing and passive, her concerns are limited to the domestic circle and to caring for others.

WHO IS JUSTINE MORITZ?

- Justine is a servant to the Frankenstein family.
- The monster sets her up as William's murderer; she is convicted and executed.

JUSTINE AND THE WILL OF HEAVEN

Justine is the most passive of all the women in the novel, often appearing to have little character of her own in the way she attempts to mimic and mirror Caroline. She is somewhat **ironically** named, given that Justine means 'righteous' or 'fair': her fate is anything but just. While so unfairly dealt with, however, she is the only character in the novel's entirely secular world to call upon God. Resigned to her fate, she even exhorts Elizabeth to learn to commit herself to the 'will of heaven' (p. 89). The life of women in *Frankenstein* does frequently seem extremely limited: they are rescued, they suffer and they die; if they are good, they are completely resigned to their lot.

CHECK THE BOOK **A04**

A useful source of information on the literary and cultural contexts of *Frankenstein* and its reception is Tim Morton's *A Routledge Literary Sourcebook on Mary Shelley's Frankenstein* (Routledge, 2002).

STUDY FOCUS: CLASS ISSUES **A02**

Caroline Frankenstein singles out and becomes very fond of both Elizabeth and Justine. It is, however, significant that Elizabeth, 'daughter of a Milanese nobleman' (p. 36), becomes an 'inmate' (p. 37) and Victor's much adored companion, while Justine, who belongs to the 'lower orders' (p. 66), is taught 'the duties of a servant' (p. 66). Look at the **narratives** describing the events leading up to the girls being taken in by Caroline (Volume One, Chapter I, pp. 36–7 and Volume One, Chapter VI, pp. 66–7), paying particular attention to language which suggests class issues.

KEY QUOTATIONS: ELIZABETH AND JUSTINE **A01**

- Victor on Elizabeth: 'The saintly soul of Elizabeth shone like a shrine-dedicated lamp in our peaceful home' (p. 39).
- Justine to Elizabeth before execution: 'Learn from me, dear lady, to submit in patience to the will of heaven!' (p. 89).

SAFIE, THE DE LACEYS AND HENRY CLERVAL

WHO IS SAFIE?

- Safie is the daughter of a Turkish merchant and a Christian Arab slave.
- She is given refuge by the De Laceys when her father plans to take her to Turkey.

THE INDEPENDENT WOMAN

Through the more positive representation of Safie, Shelley critiques the idealisation and spiritualisation of women. Like Caroline, Safie's mother is rescued by a man; in her case, however, it is more obviously an exchange of one form of slavery for another and she rejects both. Instead of resigning herself to a life-long devotion to her deliverer, she fosters rebellion in her daughter Safie by teaching her to aspire to 'higher powers of intellect and an independence of spirit' (p. 127). Consquently, Safie is less than pleased at the prospect of being locked away in a harem, 'allowed only to occupy herself with infantile amusements' (p. 127). This situation might hold a certain charm for Elizabeth. While Safie possesses feminine qualities of gentleness and affection, unlike Elizabeth she combines these with masculine qualities of independence and action. Not content to wait for rescue, she defies parental and social tyranny and makes the trip to Germany on her own.

WHO ARE THE DE LACEYS?

- The De Lacey family includes the blind father, his son, Felix, and his daughter, Agatha.
- The monster takes secret refuge in a hovel adjoining their cottage in Germany. He gains an education listening to them teaching Safie.
- The De Laceys repulse the monster when he reveals himself to them, and in revenge he burns down their cottage.

PARAGONS OF VIRTUE?

The members of the De Lacey family initially appear to be paragons of virtue: noble, hard-working, pure of heart, affectionate and moral. By showing these splendid qualities to be of little help to them when forced into conflict with more unscrupulous characters – they get thrown into prison – Shelley suggests it will take more than a few virtuous individuals to challenge a powerful and corrupt society. It is also significant that, no matter how good or benevolent these characters may be, they immediately reject the monster when they see him. Prejudice against the alien, against what is physically different, is shown to be pervasive even among these supposedly most charitable of beings.

WHO IS HENRY CLERVAL?

- Clerval is a childhood friend of Victor and Elizabeth.
- He is murdered by the monster when Victor destroys the monster's female companion.

A CONTRAST TO VICTOR

If Walton duplicates Victor in many ways, Clerval serves as Victor's opposite. He is a balanced character, an idealised form of a **Romantic** poet, and combines masculine ambition and independence with feminine gentleness, affection and sensitivity. He prefers the softer landscapes, unlike Victor, who is linked with the grandeur and isolation of mountain peaks. Clerval prefers the Persian and Arabic tales of fancy and passion to the 'heroical poetry of Greece and Rome' (p. 70). As much as anyone can, he calls forth the better feelings of Victor's heart.

THEMES

CREATION AND DIVINE ASPIRATIONS

In giving life to his creature, Victor usurps the role of God, and in her 1831 Introduction, Mary Shelley suggests that this is his main crime: his 'frightful' (p. 9) presumption in aspiring to act like God. When the story was adapted for the stage in 1823, such a reading was emphasised by the play being given the title *Presumption; or, The Fate of Frankenstein*. Nevertheless, the world Shelley creates is entirely secular: Christian myth serves only to provide **analogies** and **allusions**. There is no vengeful God to punish Victor, only a vengeful monster. Perhaps the crime upon which Shelley focuses is not so much what Victor does, but what he fails to do: nurture his creation. Victor's ambition and achievement may well be heroic; chaos ensues because he is incapable of bearing responsibility for what he produces. On the other hand, Victor's description of his 'secret toil' (p. 55) does suggest he is engaged in something shameful or unlawful.

STUDY FOCUS: A 'BIRTH MYTH' A02

Frankenstein also seeks to usurp the power of women, and in this he may be revealing his rebellion against the normal family unit and the responsibilities involved in it. Mothers are notably absent in this text, and those that appear tend to be killed rather quickly. Early feminist critics such as Ellen Moers read *Frankenstein* as a 'birth myth' which reveals a fear of the natural processes of birth, echoing Shelley's own **ambivalence** about childbirth. First pregnant at sixteen, and almost constantly pregnant during the next five years, Shelley lost most of her children soon after they were born. Later critics have found this biographical approach too reductive. It is more useful to consider the language of 'labour' and the horror in the description of Frankenstein's workshop (p. 55) as revealing something about the character of Victor, and not about the author. Consider other words and phrases in the description of Victor's creation that may suggest the idea of childbirth.

KEY QUOTATIONS: VICTOR'S WORK A01

- Victor's ambition: 'A new species would bless me as its creator and … No father could claim the gratitude of his child so completely as I should deserve theirs' (p. 55).
- Victor's description of his work and workshop: 'the moon gazed on my midnight labours … my workshop of filthy creation' (p. 55).

ISOLATION

Isolation is a key theme from the very opening, with Walton's complaints to his sister about his lack of companionship. The sufferings of both Victor and the monster are primarily caused by their alienation from others. The monster's isolation is imposed upon him by the creator who abandons him and the people who shun him. He longs for companionship and affection, and his unhappiness and subsequent violence result from his awareness that he will never experience love. Victor insists that his isolation is imposed because of the monster's crimes: he must be an outcast. Nevertheless, he chooses to isolate himself from family and friends to carry out his scientific experiments.

KEY QUOTATIONS: ISOLATION A01

- Walton's constant complaint to his sister: 'I bitterly feel the want of a friend' (p. 19).
- The monster's explanation of his behaviour: 'I am malicious because I am miserable' (p. 147).

THE FAMILY

Percy Shelley's 1818 Preface claims that the chief concern of the novel is 'the exhibition of the amiableness of domestic affection, and the excellence of universal virtue' (p. 12): domesticity is indeed frequently idealised. It is the domestic affections for which the monster longs and that Victor repeatedly holds up as the ideal to which he should have aspired. The home is represented as a paradise, the woman as the presiding angel.

Nevertheless, as Kate Ellis has convincingly argued (Kate Ellis, 'Monsters in the Garden', 1979), it is possible to read the novel as questioning the value of the domestic affections and as an attack on, rather than a celebration of, the institution of the family. Strictly enforced artificial role distinctions, Shelley demonstrates, result in the creation of a passive, dependent woman who ultimately becomes the monster who must be rejected, and like the monster, no longer the slave but the master. Victor needs to escape the 'silken cord' (p. 35) of the home in order to fulfil his desires; there is no room for ambition or individualism in the domestic world.

The treatment of the monster by the De Lacey household points to another defect in the domestic world: its insularity. Ideal though this family may seem, it functions only by excluding anything that appears as a threat to its security. The monster devotes himself to the destruction of ideal domesticity once he recognises he is doomed to be excluded from it, and in this he may be acting as Victor's **double**.

CRITICAL VIEWPOINT A03

A number of critics have noted that the window in *Frankenstein* functions much like a mirror, showing the demonic double of the self.

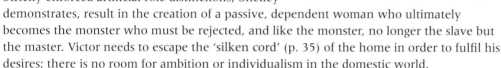

KEY QUOTATIONS: FAMILY — A01

- Victor overstating the case for the domestic affections: 'if no man allowed any pursuit whatsoever to interfere with the tranquillity of his domestic affections, Greece had not been enslaved; Caesar would have spared his country …' (p. 56).
- The monster's recognition of his lack of family: 'No father had watched my infant days, no mother had blessed me with smiles or caresses' (p. 124).

THE DOUBLE

The double or *doppelgänger* (German, literal translation is 'double walker') is a particularly common trope in nineteenth-century **Gothic**. As an externalisation of a part of the self, it is often used to demonstrate the tension between the laws of society and the desires of the individual, and to give voice to that which has been silenced by rational discourse.

The popular tendency to refer to the monster as Frankenstein is appropriate considering Shelley's use of the motif of the double. When he refers to the monster as 'my own spirit' (p. 78), Victor provides the clearest expression of the notion that he and the monster may be doubles, with the monster acting out Victor's own aggressions.

CHECK THE BOOK A03

Shelley exploits the motif of the double in some of her short stories: 'Transformation' (1831) is a Gothic fairy tale that focuses upon a deformed satanic dwarf who exchanges identities with a vindictive and dissolute youth, and 'The Mourner' (1830) considers monstrosity, the double and family relationships.

KEY QUOTATIONS: THE DOUBLE — A01

- Victor on the monster: 'my own vampire, my own spirit let loose from the grave, and forced to destroy all that was dear to me' (p. 78).
- Victor describing himself in monstrous terms: 'the only unquiet thing that wanders restless in a scene so beautiful and heavenly' (p. 94).

CRITICAL VIEWPOINT **A04**

Donna Heiland argues that **Gothic** plots are not merely plots of transgression, but also plots of gender anxiety. 'The transgressive acts at the heart of gothic fiction generally focus on corruption in, or resistance to, the patriarchal structures that shaped the country's political life and its family life, and gender roles within those structures come in for particular scrutiny' (Donna Heiland, *Gothic and Gender*, Blackwell, 2004, p. 5).

CHECK THE BOOK **A03**

The male fear of female sexuality is one of the issues addressed by Anne Mellor in *Mary Shelley: Her Life, Her Fiction and Her Monsters* (1988).

FEAR OF SEXUALITY

In creating the monster and usurping the role of woman, we could argue that Victor is rejecting human sexuality. His terrible nightmare after the creation of the monster seems to support the idea that Victor is repelled by his sexuality. When he attempts to kiss Elizabeth, she turns into a corpse, the corpse of Victor's mother, perhaps indicating also that Victor is frightened by incestuous desires. He responds to his father's suggestions that he marry with horror and dismay, and while he explains that this is because the threat of the monster still hangs over him, other readings are certainly possible. The same may be said of his words to Elizabeth on their wedding night: 'Oh! peace, peace, my love,' he tells her, 'this night, and all will be safe: but this night is dreadful, very dreadful' (p. 198).

It is also difficult to imagine how Victor could possibly misinterpret the monster's threat: 'I shall be with you on your wedding-night' (p. 173). Since it is uttered soon after Victor destroys the female companion, to the reader it seems quite clear that the threat is to Elizabeth, and yet Victor interprets it as a threat against him, and he leaves Elizabeth, on the pretext of saving her from the sight of the combat he expects, alone in the bedroom to be murdered by the monster. Here the notion of the **double** again aids in interpretation. It is possible to see the ugliness of the monster as an externalisation of Victor's destructive sexual impulses. The monster assures Victor that he will be with him on his wedding night, the time when Victor can no longer avoid confronting his own sexuality. He leaves Elizabeth alone, but the part of himself he rejects, his sexuality, does not disappear. Instead, it turns destructive and he unleashes upon her this ugly violent thing: the embodiment of his twisted sexual impulses.

KEY QUOTATIONS: VICTOR'S FEARS **A01**

- Victor's dream: 'as I imprinted the first kiss on her lips, they became livid with the hue of death' (p. 59).
- Victor considering marriage: 'Alas! to me the idea of an immediate union with my Elizabeth was one of horror and dismay' (p. 157).
- The monster's threat: 'I shall be with you on your wedding-night' (p. 173).

CRITIQUE OF SOCIETY

While the family is the institution most thoroughly examined and analysed, throughout *Frankenstein* there is a more general challenge to and criticism of the established social order and its institutions. In the story of the De Laceys, in the treatment of the monster, and in the trial of Justine, human injustice is emphasised, and the idea that society itself is monstrous is one of the key themes of the novel. Social institutions such as the law and the Church are repeatedly shown to be corrupt. Shelley frequently uses the monster as her mouthpiece in her critique of oppression and inequality in society. From his own experiences and those of the De Lacey family, the monster learns much about social injustice, and provides some pointed economic critiques. He sees how 'high and unsullied descent united with riches' (p. 123) are the possessions esteemed above all.

KEY QUOTATIONS: THE SOCIAL ORDER **A01**

- Elizabeth after the execution of Justine: 'men appear to me as monsters thirsting for each other's blood' (p. 95).
- The monster to Walton: 'Am I to be thought the only criminal, when all human kind sinned against me?' (p. 224).

THE MONSTROUS AND THE HUMAN

EARLY MONSTERS

While the term monster is often used to describe anything horrifyingly unnatural or excessively large, it initially had far more precise connotations, and these are of some significance for the ways in which the monstrous comes to function within the Gothic. Etymologically speaking, the monster is something to be shown, something that serves to demonstrate (Latin, *monstrare*: to demonstrate) and to warn (Latin, *monere*: to warn). From classical times to the Renaissance, monsters were interpreted either as signs of divine anger or portents of impending disasters. The horrific appearance of the monster gradually began to serve an increasingly moral function. By providing a visible warning of the results of vice and folly, monsters came to promote virtuous behaviour.

As an example, consider the emphasis on the monstrous as a visual warning in Shakespeare's *Macbeth* where Macduff taunts Macbeth as he attempts to withdraw from their confrontation:

Then yield thee, coward,
And live to be the show and gaze o' th' time:
We'll have thee, as our rarer monsters are,
Painted upon a pole, and underwrit
'Here may you see the tyrant.' (V.8.23–7)

STUDY FOCUS: GOTHIC MONSTERS A02

In most Gothic fiction of the eighteenth and nineteenth centuries, the monster is admitted to the text only to be ultimately expelled or repudiated. Limits and boundaries are reinstated as the monster is dispatched, good is distinguished from evil and self from **'other'**. In more recent Gothic fiction, however, monstrous figures are increasingly those with which we identify, and it is the systems that persecute these figures that come to be seen as monstrous. This is something frequently found, for example, in the stories of Angela Carter. *Frankenstein* provides a very early example of this tendency, by inviting some sympathy for the monster, allowing him to speak and explaining the origins of his behaviour. This does not happen in the other major Gothic texts of the century, and certainly not in Bram Stoker's *Dracula* (1897) where the monstrous vampire has no voice and attracts no sympathy.

MONSTROUS OR HUMAN?

Through difference, whether in appearance or behaviour, monsters function to define and construct the 'normal'. Located at the margins of culture, they police the boundaries of the human, pointing to those lines that must not be crossed. We might, for example, refer to a serial killer as a monster; the Western media frequently apply the term to people who commit terrible crimes: the point is to distance us (the human) from them (the monstrous).

Shelley's novel certainly makes any clear distinction between monstrosity and humanity problematic. If the monster's appearance is a visible warning, it is primarily a warning against the folly demonstrated by Victor. And although the monster's exterior may be horrific, he is, at least initially, certainly not frighteningly unnatural; rather, he could be seen as far more natural and humane than the creator–father who rejects him, the villagers

---

CONTEXT A04

In classical myth, monsters are frequently constructed out of ill-assorted parts, like the griffin, with the head and wings of an eagle combined with the body and paws of a lion. Victor's monster continues this tradition in being constructed out of parts taken from graves, dissecting rooms and slaughter houses.

CRITICAL VIEWPOINT A03

Christopher Craft suggests that Gothic fictions of the nineteenth century have a three-part structure. The text 'first invites or admits a monster, then entertains and is entertained by monstrosity for some extended duration, until in its closing pages it expels or repudiates the monster and all the disruptions that he/she/it brings' (Christopher Craft, 'Kiss Me with Those Red Lips', *Representations*, 8, 1984, p. 167).

who stone him or the ungrateful peasant who shoots him. It is only when he is exposed to, and suffers from, the viciousness of human society that he himself begins to demonstrate violent behaviour, to act as the monster his appearance suggests him to be. Shelley's main concern in terms of monstrosity, then, is to show the process by which human beings both create and become monsters.

Then again, from what we have seen of his treatment at the hands of ordinary humans up until this point, we might also say that the monster's new 'monstrous' behaviour is quite generally characteristic of the 'human', and not just displayed by the oppressed. It is significant that it is the decision of society's leaders to execute Justine that causes Elizabeth to declare how, in their violence and cruelty, people appear to be 'monsters thirsting for each other's blood' (p. 95). What, Shelley forces us to ask, is a monster? How do we define the monstrous, and how the human? Can we even make a clear distinction between the two, or is the monstrous rather a part of the human?

NAMING THE UNNAMEABLE

As a rational and eloquent being, Victor's creation blurs distinctions between the human and the non-human. So when we are discussing him, what do we call him? To call him, in what has become the accepted manner, the 'monster' is problematic; we need to recognise that in so doing we may in part be assuming the perspective of Victor Frankenstein and all the other characters who reject him in horror simply on the basis of his frightening appearance. On the other hand, to call him the 'creature' is to avoid the recognition that he does, in fact, become monstrous once he is rejected and is set upon revenge. If we condemn Victor for not nurturing his 'child', we also have to recognise that this 'child' responds to rejection by murdering little William and framing the innocent Justine. We can condemn the way others treat him, but we cannot condone the way he then treats others.

REVISION FOCUS: TASK 5 A02

How far do you agree with the statement below?

● Shelley's monster is a sympathetic figure.

Try writing an opening paragraph for an essay based on this discussion point. Set out your arguments clearly.

STRUCTURE

NARRATIVE STRUCTURE

The complex narrative structure of *Frankenstein* involves **framed** or **embedded narratives** – what has been called a Chinese box or Russian doll structure of stories within stories, that looks something like this:

[Robert Walton [Victor Frankenstein [Monster] Victor Frankenstein] Robert Walton]

In the outermost frame narrative, Walton writes to his sister, Mrs Margaret Saville, in England. At this stage, we have an **epistolary** narrative. This is dropped as we move to an embedded narrative: Victor's account of his life. Victor's narrative serves to frame the creature's embedded narrative at the very heart of the text. He recounts his tale, and that of the De Lacey family, to Victor, who in turn recounts it to Walton. The narrative then returns to Frankenstein until the final chapter, when Walton again takes over, and we return to the frame narrative for the conclusion of the story. The anarchic energy of the text, we could say, is formally restrained by this tight structure.

> **CHECK THE BOOK** **A02**
>
> Emily Brontë's *Wuthering Heights* (1847) is another nineteenth-century novel with a similarly complicated and tight narrative structure enclosing the anarchic rebellions of the characters against the established order.

STRUCTURAL CONNECTIONS

The problem with using the Chinese box or Russian doll **analogy** to describe the structure of *Frankenstein* is that this term tends to suggest that each story is entirely separate, complete in itself. The narratives are neither **linear** nor complete, however; we are not taken directly from the beginning of one narrator's tale to the end and then move to the next **narrator's** tale. To give an example, Walton's initial narrative provides us with an account of Victor's predicament that would, in a linear narrative, come near the end of Victor's narration. The novel begins in *media res*, that is, in the middle of things, and then moves into a series of flashbacks. The narratives, then, rather than being complete and whole in themselves, are interrelated and interdependent.

STUDY FOCUS: SHIFTING POINT OF VIEW   **A02**

As David Lodge observes, 'there is no rule or regulation that says a novel may not shift its point of view whenever the writer chooses; but if it is not done according to some aesthetic plan or principle, the reader's involvement, the reader's "production" of the meaning of the text, will be disturbed' (*The Art of Fiction*, 1993, p. 28). The changes in point of view must, then, have some function. Do you think there is an identifiable 'aesthetic plan or principle' underlying the various shifts in narrative perspective found in *Frankenstein*? To what extent does each shift in point of view – Walton to Victor to monster – contribute to the production of the meaning of the text?

FORM

NARRATION

The **convention** of a **frame narrative** is that we accept that the story contained within it is remembered and transcribed virtually word for word by the frame **narrator**. We might, then, ask to what degree differences in **voice** are removed by this process, if voice is considered in its vague sense of the distinctive features of **tone** and style. Is the voice in the monster's narrative all that distinct from that in Walton's or Victor's? Are there discernible differences which help to express unique personalities, or are the markers which would allow us to distinguish between narrators lost by the frame narrator's recounting of the other stories, or perhaps by Victor correcting and 'augmenting' the manuscript (p. 213)?

STUDY FOCUS: THE NARRATEE · A02

The **narratee**, as David Lodge defines it, is 'any evocation of, or surrogate for, the reader of the novel within the text itself' (*The Art of Fiction*, 1993, p. 80). The structure of *Frankenstein* draws attention to the presence of a listener or narratee for each narrator and this encourages the reader to consider what purpose each narrator has in speaking, what influence he is attempting to exert over the narratee, and also to assess the extent to which the response of the narratee seems reasonable.

NARRATIVE CONNECTIONS

The narrative style additionally invites us to look for echoes and **parallels** which link the stories together and simultaneously to identify differences between the three characters. Walton's ambitions, for example, make him a potential Frankenstein, and he too is isolated and alienated from the domestic world. However, Walton truly seems to long for the affection and companionship that Victor spurns, and in this sense he is more closely linked to the monster. In addition, no matter how alienated Walton may feel in the icy wastes of the Arctic, he has his crew, a community of sorts who prevent him from indulging in the kind of rampant individualism that destroys Victor.

THE UNRELIABLE NARRATOR

We might also consider how reliable the narrators are, both in their assessment of themselves and in their interpretation of other characters and situations. When Victor compares his feelings to those of Justine, condemned to be executed, and assures us that the 'tortures of the accused did not equal mine' (p. 86), do we perhaps feel that he is a little too self-absorbed to be the best interpreter of other people's feelings? Does Victor even really understand his own fears? He tells us he does not want to rush into marriage with Elizabeth because he has to deal with the monster, but his dreams suggest there is more to it than this: he would rather dabble with test tubes than procreate in the normal way.

NARRATIVE CLOSURE

Finally, we need to consider whether there is narrative **closure** or if the novel remains open-ended. As it is so difficult to fix one meaning or message to Shelley's *Frankenstein*, then on the level of interpretation there is no closure. Although we seem to come to a decisive end with the death of Victor and Walton's decision to return home, there is actually no real closure on the level of plot either. The monster vows to destroy himself. As Fred Botting points out, however, 'from the textual evidence the reader can never know what happens to the monster' (*Making Monstrous*, 1991, p. 43). This ending is forever deferred, something projected in the future, and Shelley leaves us, like the monster, 'lost in darkness and distance' (p. 225).

THE GOTHIC

In her 1831 Introduction, Shelley declares her desire to 'curdle the blood, and quicken the beatings of the heart' (p. 8). This is the first of many signals to the reader that *Frankenstein* should be placed in the **genre** of the **Gothic**. In spite of Shelley's claim to be writing a 'ghost story', however, there is nothing supernatural here; it is an emphatically secular and material world that she creates. There are no decaying monasteries, no decadent monks, headless nuns, nor terrifying brigands; castles are mentioned as though features of a travelogue rather than serving as the setting for supernatural events. All the conventional Gothic trappings have disappeared.

GOTHIC PARODY

In 1818, when *Frankenstein* first appeared, the publication of Jane Austen's **parody**, *Northanger Abbey*, suggested that the Gothic genre, once so popular it dominated the novel market, had become too formulaic and was losing credibility. Austen's heroine is so immersed in these Gothic fictions that she interprets all her experiences in terms of their **conventions**. Austen, criticising her heroine's over-stimulated imagination, points to some of the new directions that Gothic will take by bringing horror home to England and simultaneously showing that real terror is produced in and by the mind, not by haunted castles and apparitions wandering through the night.

PRECURSORS OF THE GOTHIC

While what we call the Gothic emerged in the eighteenth century as a response to, or product of, Enlightenment rationalism, it is of course possible to identify earlier texts with interests in transgression, the supernatural, and so on. Elizabethan and Jacobean revenge tragedies such as John Webster's *The White Devil* (1612) or Middleton's and Rowley's *The Changeling* (1622), for example, exerted a great deal of influence on the figure of the Gothic villain.

However, in considering earlier texts as precursors of the Gothic, we must be careful to recognise the very different contexts in which they were produced and received. Chaucer's 'Pardoner's Tale' may be a story about death but, emerging from a world in which the Black Death, the plague, was a constant fear, it is very different in its approach to *Frankenstein*, which reacts to the grim materiality of death with frightful visions of rotting shrouds and grave worms.

Shakespeare was an important model for many Gothic novelists, associated by Ann Radcliffe and others with ideas of **sublime** terror. Furthermore, as Dale Townshend notes, Shakespeare provided the Gothic writers of the eighteenth century with a model for connecting ghost-seeing with guilt (John Drakakis and Dale Townshend, eds., *Gothic Shakespeare*, 2008, p. 45). In *Macbeth*, for example, Macbeth's perception of the ghost of Banquo (III.4) can be seen as the externalised projection of a guilty conscience. By the late eighteenth and early nineteenth centuries, as we see in *Frankenstein*, the spectral and monstrous have become the externalised projection of even more complex repressed anxieties and desires.

CHECK THE BOOK **A04**

The Gothic (2003), by David Punter and Glennis Byron provides a useful introduction to this genre.

GRADE BOOSTER **A02**

If you are studying *Frankenstein* for an AQA/B examination, you must be able to assess the position of the novel within the Gothic. More generally, understanding how form and genre work is essential for AO2 across all boards.

CRITICAL VIEWPOINT **A02**

With the increasing emphasis on the haunted consciousness, the gloom and horror of Gothic landscapes become markers of internal psychological states rather than embodiments of external threats.

STUDY FOCUS: HAUNTED MINDS   A02

With the rise of the forces of secularisation and scepticism during the Enlightenment, there was a strong rationalist movement towards discrediting supernatural phenomena with things like phantasmagorias – public entertainments in which ghosts were created with the use of a magic lantern and displayed as optical illusions. Ghosts became entertainment, spectacle, and were disconnected from ideas of religion, from issues of scepticism and belief.

According to Freud, what the mind rejects in one form will probably return to haunt it in another, and, as Terry Castle argues in *The Female Thermometer* (1995), this is exactly what happened with regard to ghosts: they moved into the spaces of the mind. The haunted castle was replaced by the haunted consciousness. It is only after this that we begin to speak of being 'haunted by a thought'. How are these changes evident in *Frankenstein*? You will notice there are no ghosts here, no spirits in the traditional sense, and yet Victor frequently speaks of himself using spectral **metaphors**, for example, when he speaks of being the only 'unquiet thing that wandered restless' (p. 94). In a sense, Victor Frankenstein can be said to embody the new haunted consciousness of the age. As the American poet Emily Dickinson was to put it later in the nineteenth century, 'One need not be a chamber to be haunted …'.

CONTEXT   A04

In 2006, Tate Britain staged a re-creation of 'The Phantasmagoria' as part of its exhibition 'Gothic Nightmares: Fuseli, Blake and the Romantic Imagination'.

GOTHIC *FRANKENSTEIN*

Reading *Frankenstein* as a **Gothic** novel, we might suggest that what Victor does and what Victor creates are unnatural. He goes too far, breaks the laws of nature, crosses forbidden boundaries, and he unleashes, within himself and in society, disruption and destruction. *Frankenstein* quite clearly fits within modern conceptions of the Gothic: with its suggestions of incest in Victor's love for his 'more than sister' (p. 37) Elizabeth; with the focus on a creative act that usurps the natural functions of both God and women and a creation that blurs the boundaries between life and death; and with the allowance for the possibility that the creature is Victor's **doppelgänger**, acting out his forbidden desires and expressing the darker side of his psyche.

FRANKENSTEIN AS PRECURSOR OF LATER GOTHIC FICTIONS

CHECK THE BOOK   A03

Angela Carter continues the Gothic interests in the transgressive with 'The Snow Child' (*The Bloody Chamber*, 1979), a complex tale of incestuous rape and sexual rivalry.

In its exploration of these concepts, its focus on the dark side of the psyche, *Frankenstein* also begins to emerge as a precursor of such later Victorian Gothic novels as Stevenson's *Dr Jekyll and Mr Hyde* (1886), Wells's *The Island of Dr Moreau* (1896) and Wilde's *The Picture of Dorian Gray* (1890). Like *Frankenstein*, these novels refuse to distance the reader from the horrors described but insist instead on the modernity of the setting and the concerns; they draw on science, not superstition, on what is frighteningly possible and familiar rather than entirely absurd and alien. They make an inescapable link between the world of the text and the world of the reader.

REVISION FOCUS: TASK 6   A01

How far do you agree with the statement below?

● In *Frankenstein*, the supernatural functions metaphorically to reveal a state of mind.

Try writing an opening paragraph for an essay based on this discussion point. Set out your arguments clearly.

THE ROMANTIC MOVEMENT

Frankenstein may be primarily a Gothic novel, but as the many quotations from poets such as Coleridge suggest, the novel has significant connections with the **Romantic** movement. The link seems almost inevitable, given Mary's family background. Her father, Godwin, had a notable impact on many of the English Romantic poets and is mentioned frequently in their writings. Her husband, Percy Bysshe Shelley, was one of the key Romantic poets, and Mary was frequently in the company of such other notable Romantics as Lord Byron. While the influence of Romanticism on Mary Shelley is undeniable, it is nevertheless not quite so easy to decide what stand she is taking on the Romantic concerns that pervade *Frankenstein*. While in the past critics have gone so far as to call *Frankenstein* a handbook of Romanticism, they now frequently tend to see the novel more as a critique than a celebration of Romantic ideals.

Romanticism is as difficult to define as the Gothic. Nevertheless, there are at least three defining characteristics which can be identified with some confidence as features of Romanticism that are also of specific relevance to Shelley's *Frankenstein*. There is a concern with radical social reform, a preoccupation with the role of the poet and the workings of the imagination, and an interest in nature.

ROMANTICISM AND REFORM

The Romantic movement is usually considered to originate around 1789, the year of the French Revolution, which was initially seen by many Romantic poets as the beginnings of a new age of justice and equality. Most became disillusioned about the possibilities of reform through political action, and while *Frankenstein* is concerned with the corruption of social institutions, Shelley shows little faith in the possibility of change.

In their championing of social progressive causes and their rejection of conventional social morals, many Romantics felt isolated, alienated from society as a whole. For the Romantics, the imagination is used both to escape the world and to transform it. Such creativity is seen as powerful, God-like, leading to an emphasis on the assertion of the self and the value of individual experience. They become Promethean figures – in this respect like Victor, as the subtitle suggests – who rival and defy God himself, creating the world anew through poetry.

NATURE AND THE SUBLIME

As the Romantics looked within to their own inner natures, they also looked without to the natural world around them. Reacting against the earlier eighteenth-century admiration for the ordered and cultivated, they became more interested in the wild and untamed aspects of nature. In this respect they were greatly influenced by Edmund Burke (1729–97) and his *Philosophical Enquiry into the Origin of Our Ideas of the Sublime and the Beautiful* (1757). Burke defined the beautiful as that characterised by smallness, orderliness, smoothness, brightness; the **sublime**, however, was of much more interest to the Romantics, with its associations of darkness, solitude, infinity, of terror inspired by the gigantic and incomprehensible that ultimately led to an elevation of the self.

STUDY FOCUS: THE SUBLIME LANDSCSAPE **A02**

While Shelley provides many sublime landscapes, it is difficult to decide whether or not she is celebrating them in the Romantic manner. Her characters may, but does she? Is there inspiration in the icy mountainous landscape where Victor confronts the creature, in the Orkneys where he begins to make the companion, and in the Arctic regions where both meet their deaths? Or do these sublime landscapes simply seem dangerous, alien, sterile? Do they stimulate and inspire or do they suggest alienation and the death of feeling? Perhaps these alien and barren landscapes have no more to do with humanity than Victor's egotistical Promethean desires.

CONTEXT **A02**

Walton's language frequently echoes that of the Romantic poets. When he concludes, for example, 'My swelling heart involuntarily pours itself out thus' (p. 24), his effusions could be seen to suggest Wordsworth's famous lines from the Preface to the *Lyrical Ballads* (1802): 'poetry is the spontaneous overflow of powerful feelings: it takes its origin from emotion recollected in tranquillity'.

CHECK THE BOOK **A04**

For a useful introduction to the Romantic movement, see Marilyn Butler, *Romantics, Rebels and Reactionaries: English Literature and Its Background* (Oxford University Press, 1981).

CONTEXT **A04**

The sublime is particularly associated with the seventeenth-century Italian landscape painter Salvator Rosa. His trademark jagged mountains and stormy skies can be seen in such paintings as *Landscape with a Hermit* (c. 1662) and *The Death of Empedocles* (1665).

LANGUAGE

THE LANGUAGE OF THE GOTHIC

In the story of *Frankenstein* there is always more emphasis on description than on dramatic action, more emphasis on telling than showing. The language is often highly emotional and **melodramatic**, threatening, some critics would say, to fall into absurdity. Indeed, much the same could be said of most eighteenth- and early nineteenth-century **Gothic** fictions. There is an emphasis on description, but this does not involve a detailed analysis of inner feeling. 'Everything internal,' George Levine claims, 'is transformed into large public gesture or high **rhetorical** argument' (George Levine, *The Endurance of Frankenstein*, 1979, p. 19). Alternatively, the inner life remains unexplored, to emerge only indirectly through **images** or dreams, through descriptions of landscape, as in Victor's various **Romantic** musings on nature. The language of the Gothic frequently is, like the themes it explores, one of excess rather than restraint – consider, for example, Victor's raging against the 'Abhorred monster' and 'fiend' (p. 102) – and in this respect it is set in structural opposition to the classical.

STUDY FOCUS: LANGUAGE AND THE SUBLIME A02

In his essay 'On the Sublime', the Ancient Greek philosopher Longinus associated the **sublime** with a style of elevated rhetoric, one that had the power to take the reader into another world. Among the main elements of the sublime for Longinus are vehement and inspired passion; noble diction (the choice and use of words); and dignified and elevated composition.

Analyse the language in Victor's description of the valley of Chamounix in Volume Two Chapter II, pp. 99–101. Initially, Victor's description may demonstrate some of the features identified by Longinus as Victor is lifted out of himself, his heart swelling 'with something like joy'. But notice how the language becomes darker with the appearance of the monster, and Victor feels faint, overcome and initially deprived of all speech. Here we see not Longinus's elevating sublime, but a Gothic sublime which only threatens the disintegration of the self.

ELOQUENCE

For first-time readers of *Frankenstein*, the monster's eloquence is a surprise. We might expect a grunting animal, but what we are confronted with, as Peter Brooks notes, is a 'supreme rhetorician of his own situation'; he controls the **antitheses** and **oxymorons** 'that express the pathos of his existence' (Peter Brooks, 'Godlike Science/Unhallowed Arts', 1979, pp. 206–7). Consider, for example, the impressive use of balance and opposition in his injunction to Victor: 'Remember, that I am thy creature; I ought to be thy Adam; but I am rather the fallen angel, whom thou drivest from joy for no misdeed. Every where I see bliss, from which I alone am irrevocably excluded. I was benevolent and good; misery made me a fiend. Make me happy, and I shall again be virtuous' (p. 103). Victor is eventually persuaded to make him a mate. Language, initially, seems to have power in this novel.

GOTHIC AND THE UNSPEAKABLE

Nevertheless, language simultaneously seems inadequate and weak. Characters repeatedly assert their inability to express their feelings in language, falling back on such phrases as 'no one can conceive' or 'I cannot describe' (e.g. pp. 21, 55, 115 and 151). This is a traditional feature of the Gothic and suggests the inadequacy of language to capture and account for inner experience. Experience, in Gothic, is more precisely captured **symbolically** in dreams. For example, the nightmare Victor experiences after bringing the monster to life, when Elizabeth is transformed into the corpse of his dead mother, tells us as post-Freudian readers all we need to know about Victor's true feelings for his mother and for Elizabeth, and all we need to know about his attitude towards human sexuality.

THE 'GODLIKE SCIENCE' OF LANGUAGE

It could be said that *Frankenstein* is all about language: its potential power and the breakdown of that power when faced with the prejudices and insensitivity of a society that tends to privilege the visual, to judge above all on appearances. The first key stage of the monster's education is his recognition of the importance of language. In the hovel adjoining the De Lacey cottage, he sees that people communicate 'their experience and feelings to one another by articulate sounds', and, even more importantly, that the words they speak 'produced pleasure or pain, smiles or sadness' (p. 115); they produce, that is, emotional effects. While aware that his physical appearance would cause only revulsion if he confronted the family, the monster believes that by becoming an adept in the 'godlike science' (p. 115) of language, he will be able through his gentle words to win their affection.

The monster's success with the blind father initially bears out his faith in language but, as soon as the others enter, the importance of appearances reasserts itself, and prejudice against what looks alien and **'other'** wins out. The monster has a similar experience in his attempt to persuade Victor to create a mate for him; once again, this is an attempt to gain love and companionship through language. Victor is indeed convinced by his eloquence: 'His words had a strange effect on me. I compassionated him' (p. 149). But the effect is fleeting: as soon as he looks upon the monster, he is again filled with horror for the 'filthy mass that moved and talked' (p. 149). When he next catches sight of this 'filthy mass' at the window of the hut where he is making the female, enough time has passed for the effects of eloquence to have worn off completely. Victor reads in the monster's countenance only malice and treachery, and he tears the female to pieces.

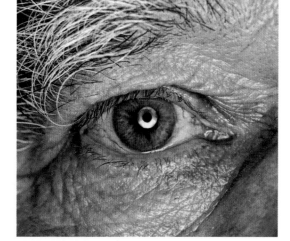

Victor too is noted for his fluency with words, his ability to manipulate language, his 'unparalleled eloquence' (p. 29). His voice, like the glittering eye of Coleridge's ancient mariner, compels the listener to attend. When he speaks, Walton notes, the sailors no longer want to return home, no longer despair; they are roused to action, filled with courage. But this does not last; the effect persists only as long as the voice is heard, and once Victor is dead, the sailors insist on Walton turning back. Victor's eloquence also impresses Walton, but, notably, this eloquence fails to persuade him to take over the quest to destroy the monster.

CHECK THE BOOK **A02**

For a useful discussion of language in *Frankenstein*, see Peter Brooks, '"Godlike Science/Unhallowed Arts": Language, Nature, and Monstrosity', 1979.

THE PROBLEM OF VOICE

Insisting on the power of the heard voice, Shelley draws our attention to the difference between reading and hearing **narratives**; we can only be told of the modulations in the voice of the speaker. It is difficult to convey, through writing, the sound of Victor's 'full-toned voice' (p. 32) whose 'varied intonations', according to Walton, are 'soul-subduing music' (p. 30). We are told the monster's voice is harsh, but we cannot hear that harshness as we read. Voice is inevitably a rather vague and not particularly useful technical term in literary studies, and distinctions between narrative voice (as opposed to **narrative point of view**) tend to be distinctions between different ways of addressing the reader; it is, clearly, far easier to determine that a voice is **ironic** or intimate than it is to determine than it is 'full-toned' or harsh.

HISTORICAL BACKGROUND

SOCIAL UNREST

Frankenstein was written at a time of great changes in British society and deals with a variety of issues central to the development of industrial Britain in the late eighteenth and early nineteenth centuries. This was a period of significant developments in science and technology and, at least partly as a result of such advances, also a time of social and political upheaval.

Technological developments had a notable impact on people's lives, endangering traditional ways of living in much the same way as scientific developments undermined traditional beliefs. In the first stages of the Industrial Revolution the introduction of new technologies posed a significant threat to the livelihoods of many of the lower classes, frequently prompting violent reactions. The Luddite disturbances of 1811–17, during which factories and mills were attacked and machines destroyed, stirred uneasy memories of the bloodier excesses of the French Revolution of 1789. William Godwin, Shelley's father, initially saw

the French Revolution as the sign of the start of a new era in history with the removal of corrupt institutions. Although its original aims were admirable, the means adopted were violent, and the revolutionaries' execution of the king, traditionally considered the representative of the divine on earth, suggested defiance of God's laws.

The Pentridge uprising of 1817, when 300 men marched towards Nottingham, expecting numerous other such marches throughout the country, was designed to overthrow the government and seemed to confirm the alarming possibility of revolt in Britain. When the leaders of the Pentridge uprising were executed in November, Percy Shelley responded with a political pamphlet deploring the state of a country torn between the alternatives of anarchy and oppression. Mary Shelley had radical sympathies and, through her depiction of the monster, she reveals an awareness of social injustice and a passionate desire for reform. At the same time, she could not fully support rebellion against the established order, and, again through the monster, expresses fear of the revolutionary violence that injustice in society might provoke.

SCIENTIFIC DEVELOPMENTS: THE LIFE-PRINCIPLE

Shelley's *Frankenstein* emerges at least partly out of her familiarity with and understanding of the scientific debates and discoveries of her time. During the later eighteenth century, traditional philosophical and theological investigations into the meaning of life began to be displaced by secular and materialist explorations of life's origins and nature. In 1771, Joseph Priestley observed that mice placed in a bell jar depleted the air and led to suffocation, while sprigs of mint refreshed the air and made the mice lively. Eight years later, Antoine Lavoisier interpreted Priestley's data to provide the first understanding of the processes of respiration. Many scientists, however, remained reluctant to accept a theory that made human life dependent upon the vegetative world: the idea that life might be either maintained or initiated simply through material causes challenged all traditional beliefs about the soul and about humanity's unique position within the world.

By 1814, a debate over what came to be known as the 'life-principle' had caused a rift in the sciences: it was encapsulated in the differing positions of John Abernethy, President of the Royal College of Surgeons, and his pupil William Lawrence, appointed as second Professor at the College in 1815. Lawrence advocated a strictly materialist position. Abernethy, wanting to retain some metaphysical elements in common with religious beliefs, argued that life could not be entirely explained in material terms; something else was required, some vital principle that might be linked to the concept of the immortal soul. In *Mary Shelley* (1988), Anne Mellor demonstrates how closely Shelley relied upon the works of Humphrey Davy, Erasmus Darwin and Luigi Galvani. Davy's pamphlet, *A Discourse, Introductory to a Course of Lectures on Chemistry* (1802), provides Shelley with information about chemistry, with the suggestion that chemistry might provide the secret of life, and with material for Waldman's lectures. Shelley, like Davy, distinguishes the master-scientist who seeks to interfere with and control nature, to modify and change nature's creations, from the scholar-scientist who seeks only to understand.

Unlike Davy, however, Shelley believed the former to be dangerous, and the latter to be the good scientist, exemplified by Erasmus Darwin. Percy Shelley, in his 1818 Preface, refers to Darwin as one of the scientists who have considered such an act of creation possible (p. 12). Darwin, however, like his better-known grandson, Charles, was an evolutionist, not a creationist. He is therefore directly opposed to the fictional Victor Frankenstein who wants to create and change life through chemical means and is not willing to wait for the slow processes of evolution. From this perspective Victor is, like Davy, the bad scientist – the one who interferes with and changes nature. Darwin is the good scientist who only observes and records.

GALVANISM

It is specifically galvanism, however, to which Mary Shelley refers in *Frankenstein*. In 1791, Luigi Galvani published *Commentary on the Effects of Electricity on Muscular Motion*, suggesting that animal tissue contained a vital force, which he dubbed 'animal electricity' but later came to be known as 'galvanism'. Galvani believed this was a different form of electricity from that produced by such things as lightning, that it was produced by the brain, conducted by the nerves, and produced muscular motion. This theory led to a variety of experiments on human corpses, the most notorious of which was carried out by Giovanni Adini on the corpse of the murderer Thomas Forster after he was hanged at Newgate. Wires were attached to stimulate galvanic activity and the corpse began to move, giving the appearance of re-animation. Such experiments as this were widely discussed in detail in the popular press, and no doubt influenced Shelley's *Frankenstein*. Drawing upon scientific research, then, Shelley provides a frighteningly believable prediction of what the future might be like in a world where humans hold the secret of life.

CONTEXT **AO4**

Percy Bysshe Shelley had a lifelong interest in science, and Dr Adam Walker, who theorised electricity as the spark of life, the soul of the material world, had a particularly strong influence upon him. Shelley conducted various experiments, which apparently led to results ranging from holes in his clothes and carpet to electrifying the family cat.

CHECK THE BOOK **AO4**

Susan Lederer's beautifully illustrated *Frankenstein: Penetrating the Secrets of Nature* (2002) offers an excellent introduction to the science of the time, and links this to our contemporary scientific concerns.

LITERARY BACKGROUND

ANALOGIES AND ALLUSIONS

Frankenstein is full of both **analogies** drawn between the characters and other figures from literature and myth and **allusions** to various other texts. Indeed, it could be said that, as the monster is constructed out of fragments of corpses, the text is constructed out of fragments of other texts. The major stories which Shelley appropriates and reworks are Milton's *Paradise Lost* (1667) and Coleridge's 'The Rime of the Ancient Mariner' (1798).

PARADISE LOST

Did I request thee, Maker, from my clay
To mould Me man? Did I solicit thee
From darkness to promote me? (*Paradise Lost*, 10.743–5)

Shelley chooses for her **epigraph** a quotation from *Paradise Lost*, one of the books in the monster's library, and this, along with the many other references to Milton's epic poem throughout the novel, suggests the need to keep this story in mind when reading *Frankenstein*. The epigraph immediately encourages us to associate Victor with God and the monster with Adam, and this seems appropriate since, as creator, Victor assumes the role of God, and the 'man' he creates is the monster. However, while the monster certainly fits the role of Adam, he also becomes the demon, assuming the role of Satan, the fallen archangel who engineers the fall of Adam and brings Sin and Death into the world. When the monster confronts Victor, after the murder of William, he declares that he has been changed by his exclusion from paradise: 'I am thy creature; I ought to be thy Adam, but I am rather the fallen angel, whom thou drivest from joy for no misdeed' (p. 103). The monster even echoes Satan's words in *Paradise Lost* at such moments as when he declares to Walton that, after his potential companion had been destroyed, 'Evil thenceforth became my good' (p. 222).

Victor similarly links himself with Satan, the fallen angel, and while the **analogy** drawn between the monster and Satan focuses attention on the creature's horrific acts of savage violence, the analogy drawn between Victor and Satan focuses attention more on Victor's pride and ambition. In attempting to displace God, he demonstrates the same pride as Satan, who had similar aspirations. Commenting upon his torment of guilt, Victor draws upon the following **simile**: 'Like the archangel who aspired to omnipotence, I am chained in an eternal hell' (p. 214). Victor's hell is within him: it is hell as a psychological state, but this is also true of the hell so powerfully described by Satan in *Paradise Lost*.

For the **Romantics**, Milton's Satan is an interesting, even glamorous figure, nothing like the shadowy figure of the Bible. Percy Shelley even considered that Satan was morally superior to God in Milton's poem, and many of the Romantic poets admired the grandeur and boldness of his aspirations. While Victor must be condemned for the neglect of his creature, it is possible that he too can still be admired for his bold aspirations, his refusal to be satisfied with a mundane and uneventful existence with his family, and his attempt to give humankind a power thought to belong to God alone. To come to that conclusion, however, perhaps we need to be convinced that his work is driven by the desire to benefit others and not by more selfish motives.

CHECK THE BOOK **A03**

For further information on the Romantic attitude to Satan, see Kenneth Gross's 'Satan and the Romantic Satan', in Margaret Ferguson and Mary Nyquist, eds., *Remembering Milton: Essays on the Texts and Traditions* (Methuen, 1987).

'THE RIME OF THE ANCIENT MARINER'

Coleridge's poem was first published in 1798 in *Lyrical Ballads*. The story concerns an ancient mariner who meets three men on their way to a wedding feast; he detains one and, with his 'glittering eye', holds him while he recounts his story. He tells how his ship was drawn towards the South Pole by a storm and the ship became surrounded by ice. In this world devoid of living things an albatross flies through the fog and the crew greets it with joy. It seems to be a good omen. The ice splits, the ship begins to move, and the bird flies along with it. Inexplicably, the mariner shoots it, and for this act of cruelty a curse descends upon the ship. She is driven towards the Equator and becalmed on a silent rotting sea under the burning sun. The dead bird is hung around the neck of the mariner. Death and Life-in-Death appear, playing dice on a skeleton ship. When it vanishes all the crew die, with the exception of the mariner; he is left alone in an alien world. Moved by the beauty of watersnakes in the moonlight, the mariner blesses them, and the albatross falls from his neck. He is saved, but, in penance, is condemned to travel the world teaching love and reverence for all God's creatures.

The most obvious connection with the story of the ancient mariner is Walton's journey into the frozen wastes of the Arctic; Walton even quotes the poem when the ship is trapped in the ice. However, the mariner's story actually seems to throw more light upon the experiences of the other characters. Like Victor, the ancient mariner defies God. In shooting the albatross he disturbs the natural order: his world, like Victor's, is transformed into a nightmare vision of an alien universe, a meaningless and terrifying wasteland, a world without God. Even after the mariner is forgiven, we are left with the suspicion that this vision of the world may have been prompted by his insight into the truth of the human condition. The monster's experiences may offer a similar insight into a godless world: an irrational, terrifying world managed only by human institutions which are corrupt and individuals who are irresponsible and cruel. Furthermore, like both Victor and the monster, the mariner is an alienated individual. Once he shoots the albatross, he is no longer at peace with himself, and he is shunned by the wider community. Even after he is forgiven, although he becomes aware of the joys of family and community life, he is forced to do penance which keeps him still a solitary, marginal figure, eternally wandering the world. The poem offers a haunting portrayal of the guilt and loneliness that Shelley also captures through the experiences of her characters.

CRITICAL VIEWPOINT A03

'An adequate reading of a literary or other cultural text will need to recognize the significance of the ways it interacts with earlier texts. This involves trying to work out the similarities and differences between the two texts that are momentarily brought together by an allusion' (Martin Montgomery et al., *Ways of Reading*, 1992, p. 159).

CRITICAL DEBATES

ORIGINAL RECEPTION

When *Frankenstein* was first published anonymously in 1818, it was extensively reviewed by many of the important journals of the time. These reviews are notable for three main points. First, most critics simply assumed the author to be a man. The eventual discovery that it was Mary Shelley caused some consternation: the blasphemous ideas expressed were considered particularly unseemly for a woman. Secondly, the style of the novel was generally praised: most agreed with *Blackwood's* (March 1818) assessment of 'the author's original genius and happy power of expression'. Finally, while being impressed by the power and vigour of the work, many reviewers criticised the subject matter and the author's refusal to moralise about Frankenstein's blasphemous act. *The Quarterly Review* of January 1818 provides a typical complaint. After summarising the plot and declaring it to be a 'tissue of horrible and disgusting absurdity', the reviewer concludes: 'Our taste and our judgement alike revolt at this kind of writing, and the greater the ability with which it may be executed the worse it is – it inculcates no lesson of conduct, manners, or morality.'

A MINOR WORK

For much of the twentieth century, *Frankenstein* was considered an interesting novel but by no means 'great literature'. In *Mary Shelley: A Biography*, R. Glynn Grylls, writing in 1938, considered it to be 'a "period piece," of not very good date; historically interesting, but not one of the living novels of the world' (p. 320). It was generally agreed to be a minor work, relegated to the margins of 'popular' literature and granted even this status only because of Mary Shelley's impressive literary relations. *Frankenstein* was considered of some importance primarily because, the general consensus was, it encapsulated in a conveniently simple form the preoccupations of **Romanticism**.

FEMINIST READINGS

Feminist Romantic scholars helped move *Frankenstein* into the spotlight by examining the relationships between the author and her fiction. Such criticism tended to focus heavily on Shelley's personal life, and, thematically, the focus was usually on her representations of motherhood and childbirth. For example, in 1974, Ellen Moers offered an influential reading of the text as a woman's mythmaking on the subject of birth ('Female Gothic' reprinted in Levine and Knoepflmacher, eds., *The Endurance of Frankenstein*, 1979). However, this kind of psycho-biographical criticism has a tendency to reduce the text to a 'monstrous' symptom of Shelley's own disturbed psyche.

RETHINKING *FRANKENSTEIN*

As the concept of a 'canon' of great works disappeared and the boundaries of 'literature' expanded, *Frankenstein* gradually began to attract more critical attention. In 1979, George Levine and U. C. Knoepflmacher edited a collection of essays, *The Endurance of Frankenstein*, that marked a turning point in *Frankenstein* criticism, and this remains one of the most useful collections available. While still convinced that *Frankenstein* was 'a "minor" novel, radically flawed by its sensationalism, by the inflexibly public and oratorical nature of even its most intimate passages', Levine argued that *Frankenstein* was the 'most important minor novel in English' (p. 3). *Frankenstein* had become a **metaphor** for our own most crucial cultural concerns, expressing the 'central dualities and tensions of our time by positing a world without God' (p. 8). Approaching the novel from a variety of critical perspectives – feminist, materialist and psychoanalytical – the essays in this collection clearly demonstrated there was far more to *Frankenstein* than a quaint perspective on

CONTEXT **A04**

'This is, perhaps, the foulest Toadstool that has yet sprung up from the reeking dunghill of the present times': comment by **Gothic** novelist William Beckford (1760–1844) scribbled on the flyleaf of his copy of the first edition of *Frankenstein*.

CRITICAL VIEWPOINT **A03**

As Shelley is sometimes seen by feminist critics to appropriate the Gothic to express anxieties associated with childbirth, so, in *Wuthering Heights*, Emily Brontë has been seen to harness the Gothic to represent women's fears about a restrictive and sometimes threatening domestic space.

Romanticism. Mary Shelley was no longer considered to be simply echoing the ideas of her more illustrious Romantic friends and relations. Instead she was seen as a woman writer offering a female perspective on such issues as birth and the family, and a female critique, rather than a celebration, of the masculine preoccupations of Romanticism.

MONSTROSITY

There has been a significant reassessment of *Frankenstein* since about 1990. New readings have stressed the significance of particular social and economic conditions to our interpretation of the text. By looking at various rewritings and reworkings of the *Frankenstein* myth, from films to cereal boxes to electricity advertisements, critics have examined the ever-changing significance of the monster and the changing cultural anxieties which he is adapted to embody. For many of the most recent critics, the text itself is 'monstrous', calling into question traditional values and comfortable categories. The idea of 'monstrosity' itself forms a key issue in Fred Botting's *Making Monstrous: Frankenstein, Criticism, Theory* (1991) which engages with both the text of *Frankenstein* and the criticism that has attempted to identify and fix the text's significance. Monstrosity is also a question with which a number of other critics engage in the essays Botting edited for the 1995 Macmillan New Casebook on *Frankenstein*. The question of whether *Frankenstein* is a 'minor' novel is no longer of any concern. This collection brings together many influential recent readings and, while the essays are often challenging, is a useful way for students to familiarise themselves with the various contemporary critical approaches to the novel.

CHECK THE BOOK A03

Johanna Smith's *Mary Shelley: Frankenstein* (2000) presents the 1831 text of Mary Shelley's novel along with critical essays from contemporary psychoanalytic, Marxist, feminist and cultural-studies perspectives. This could be of interest to those students looking to learn more about critical theory.

THE BROADER CONTEXT

The trend towards placing *Frankenstein* within a broader cultural context is reflected in Tim Marshall's *Murdering to Dissect: Grave-robbing, Frankenstein and the Anatomy Literature* (1995) and in the collection of essays, *Frankenstein, Creation, and Monstrosity*, edited by Stephen Bann (1994). *Frankenstein*'s relationship with other literary texts, including *Dracula* and *The Island of Dr Moreau*, is one focus of discussion in this collection. Other essays consider *Frankenstein* in light of the wider treatment of monstrosity in science fiction, the adaptation of text into horror film, and Shelley's treatment of magic and natural sciences.

Frankenstein also began to attract particular attention in the late twentieth century because of the increasing concerns raised by scientific research in biomedicine, including cloning and xenografting. Susan Lederer has a useful chapter on this issue in her *Frankenstein: Penetrating the Secrets of Nature* (2002), a book written to accompany a travelling exhibition of the same name.

RECENT TRENDS

Most recently, a growing field of **eco-criticism**, the study of the relationship between literature and the environment, has produced a number of new readings which draw attention to the environmental conditions of the novel, most notably the settings of the Arctic and Alps, and ask new questions about human perceptions of nature. While there are a number of academic essays on this topic, there is as yet no full-length book on eco-criticism and *Frankenstein*. Jonathan Bate's seminal eco-critical *The Song of the Earth* (2000) offers a short discussion of *Frankenstein* and is a good place to start considering these issues.

PART SIX: GRADE BOOSTER

ASSESSMENT FOCUS

WHAT ARE YOU BEING ASKED TO FOCUS ON?

The questions or tasks you are set will be based around the four **Assessment Objectives, AO1 to AO4**.

You may get more marks for certain **AOs** than others depending on which unit you're working on. Check with your teacher if you are unsure.

WHAT DO THESE AOS ACTUALLY MEAN?

ASSESSMENT OBJECTIVES	MEANING?
AO1 Articulate creative, informed and relevant responses to literary texts, using appropriate terminology and concepts, and coherent, accurate written expression.	You write about texts in accurate, clear and precise ways so that what you have to say is clear to the marker. You use literary terms (e.g. **protagonist**, **intertextuality**) or refer to concepts (e.g. **double**, **sublime**) in relevant places.
AO2 Demonstrate detailed critical understanding in analysing the ways in which structure, form and language shape meanings in literary texts.	You show that you understand the specific techniques and methods used by the writer(s) to create the text (e.g. **embedded narrative**, **metaphor**, **foreshadowing**, **pathetic fallacy**, etc.). You can explain clearly how these methods affect the meaning.
AO3 Explore connections and comparisons between different literary texts, informed by interpretations of other readers.	You are able to see relevant links between different texts. You are able to comment on how others (such as critics) view the text.
AO4 Demonstrate understanding of the significance and influence of the contexts in which literary texts are written and received.	You can explain how social, historical, political or personal backgrounds to the texts affected the writer and how the texts were read when they were first published and at different times since.

WHAT DOES THIS MEAN FOR YOUR STUDY OR REVISION?

Depending on the course you are following, you could be asked to:

- Respond to a general question about the text as a whole. For example:

Explore the ways in which Shelley exploits the sublime in *Frankenstein*.

- Write about an aspect of *Frankenstein* which is also a feature of other texts you are studying. These questions may take the form of a challenging statement or quotation which you are invited to discuss. For example:

'Gothic literature reveals both how we make and how we become monsters.' How far do you agree with this statement?

- Focus on the particular similarities, links, contrasts and differences between this text and others. For example:

Compare and contrast the use of the supernatural in *Frankenstein* and another text you have studied.

TARGETING A HIGH GRADE

It is very important to understand the progression from a lower grade to a high grade. In all cases, it is not enough simply to mention some key points and references – instead, you should explore them in depth, drawing out what is interesting and relevant to the question or issue.

TYPICAL C GRADE FEATURES

	FEATURES	EXAMPLES
A01	You use critical vocabulary accurately, and your arguments make sense, are relevant and focus on the task. You show detailed knowledge of the text.	*Robert Walton is the first narrator. His story is told in epistolary form: this means it is in a series of letters. He is writing to his sister Margaret Saville back in England.*
A02	You can say how some specific aspects of form, structure and language shape meanings.	*When the narrative perspective changes to that of the monster, we are encouraged to wonder how reliable Victor's account of events has been.*
A03	You consider in detail the connections between texts and also how interpretations of texts differ, with some relevant supporting references.	*Shelley draws on the sublime in Victor's descriptions of the awe-inspiring Alps. Jane Austen also draws on the sublime when she describes Catherine in the ball-room in Bath, but Austen's aim is parodic.*
A04	You can write about a range of contextual factors and make some specific and detailed links between these and the task or text.	*The question that preoccupies Victor, 'whence … did the principle of life proceed' (p. 52), was a matter of intense debate at the time Shelley was writing "Frankenstein".*

TYPICAL FEATURES OF AN A OR A* RESPONSE

	FEATURES	EXAMPLES
A01	You use appropriate critical vocabulary and a technically fluent style. Your arguments are well structured, coherent and always relevant, with a very sharp focus on task.	*In calling the book 'my hideous progeny' (p. 10), Shelley makes a clear connection between the text and the monster. Like the monster, the text is stitched together out of miscellaneous parts. This is evident both in the way it is compiled of various distinct narratives and in its strongly intertextual form.*
A02	You explore and analyse key aspects of form, structure and language and evaluate perceptively how they shape meanings.	*'What may not be expected in a country of eternal light?' (p. 15) Walton asks. While Walton uses the term 'light' in a literal sense here, the term also comes to assume metaphorical meaning: it is associated with discovery and knowledge, with the 'enlightenment' that both Victor and Walton seek in their different ways. For each man, however, the search for light ultimately leads only into darkness.*
A03	You show a detailed and perceptive understanding of issues raised through connections between texts and can consider different interpretations with a sharp evaluation of their strengths and weaknesses. You have a range of excellent supportive references.	*Victor's dream of embracing Elizabeth and seeing her turn into the corpse of his dead mother in his arms, with the grave worms crawling in the shroud, could be interpreted in a number of ways. On one level, as numerous critics have argued, the dream can be seen to reveal incestuous desire for the mother. On another level, it also reveals revulsion towards the materiality of the body, the inevitable physical decay, that is part of what historian Philippe Ariès has identified as a growing antipathy towards death beginning in the late eighteenth century. There is no horror expressed here; rather, death is a much-desired means of obliterating all boundaries between self and other.*
A04	You show deep, detailed and relevant understanding of how contextual factors link to the text or task.	*In her description of Victor's walking tour with Clerval, Shelley engages with the idea of nature as restorative that is so central to Romanticism. In 'Tintern Abbey', for example, Wordsworth notes how memories of the landscape have soothed him, providing 'sensations sweet' and 'tranquil restoration'. Going down the Rhine, Victor similarly speaks of drinking in a 'tranquillity', and he even quotes directly from 'Tintern Abbey'. There is, however, surely some irony in the representation of Victor's Romantic effusions about nature, given that he has just finished creating the most unnatural being of all.*

HOW TO WRITE HIGH-QUALITY RESPONSES

The quality of your writing – how you express your ideas – is vital for getting a higher grade, and AO1 and AO2 are specifically about how you respond.

FIVE KEY AREAS

The quality of your responses can be broken down into five key areas.

1. THE STRUCTURE OF YOUR ANSWER/ESSAY

- First, get **straight to the point or focus in your opening paragraph**. Use a sharp, direct first sentence that deals with a key aspect and then follow up with evidence or detailed reference.
- **Put forward an argument or point of view** (you won't **always** be able to challenge or take issue with the essay question, but generally, where you can, you are more likely to write in an interesting way).
- **Signpost your ideas** with connectives and references which help the essay flow.
- **Don't repeat points already made**, not even in the conclusion, unless you have something new to add.

TARGETING A HIGH GRADE A01

Consider the following essay question:

Discuss how the De Lacey family exemplifies the 'amiablenes of domestic affection' to which Percy Shelley refers in his Preface.

Here's an example of an opening paragraph that gets straight to the point:

> *The De Lacey family initially seems to offer the main example in Mary Shelley's "Frankenstein" of what Percy Shelley calls the 'amiableness of the domestic affection' (p. 12). Here all work and all rewards are shared equally. There is an atmosphere of mutual concern and difference, as the inclusion of the Turkish Safie seems to suggest, can be accepted. Safie, however, has beauty on her side; the monster does not. Rather than idealising this world, Shelley ultimately suggests it only survives because of its terrible insularity. The De Lacey family function only through excluding anything that appears to threaten their own personal security.*

Immediate focus on task and key words and example from text

2. USE OF TITLES, NAMES, ETC.

This is a simple, but important, tip to stay on the right side of the examiners.

- Make sure that you spell correctly the titles of the texts, chapters, authors and so on. Present them correctly too, with double quotation marks and capitals as appropriate. For example, *'In Volume One of "Frankenstein" …'*.
- Use the **full title**, unless there is a good reason not to (e.g. it's very long).
- Use the term 'text' rather than 'book' or 'story'. If you use the word 'story', the examiner may think you mean the plot/action rather than the 'text' as a whole.

EXAMINER'S TIP ✓

Answer the question set, not the question you'd like to have been asked! Examiners say that often students will be set a question on one character (for example, Elizabeth Lavenza) but end up writing almost as much about another (such as the monster). Or they write about one aspect from the question (for example, the nature of the monstrous) but ignore another (such as the nature of the human). **Stick to the question**, and answer **all parts of it**.

---

3. EFFECTIVE QUOTATIONS

Do not 'bolt on' quotations to the points you make. You will get some marks for including them, but examiners will not find your writing very fluent.

The best quotations are:

- Relevant
- Not too long
- Integrated into your argument/sentence

TARGETING A HIGH GRADE   A01

Here is an example of a quotation successfully embedded in a sentence:

Walton's exploration of the Arctic is in part a quest to conquer nature, to penetrate and 'proceed over the untamed yet obedient element' (p. 24).

Remember – quotations can be a well-selected set of three or four single words or phrases embedded in a sentence to build a picture or explanation, or they can be longer ones that are explored and picked apart.

4. TECHNIQUES AND TERMINOLOGY

By all means mention literary terms, techniques, **conventions** or people (for example, '**paradox**' or 'archetype' or 'Prometheus') **but** make sure that you:

- Understand what they mean
- Are able to link them to what you're saying
- Spell them correctly!

5. GENERAL WRITING SKILLS

Try to write in a way that sounds professional and uses standard English. This does not mean that your writing will lack personality – just that it will be authoritative.

- Avoid colloquial or everyday expressions such as 'got', 'alright', 'ok' and so on.
- Use terms such as 'convey', 'suggest', 'imply', 'infer' to explain the writer's methods.
- Refer to 'we' when discussing the audience/reader.
- Avoid assertions and generalisations; don't just state a general point of view (*The women in the text are all passive …*), but analyse closely with clear evidence and textual detail.

TARGETING A HIGH GRADE   A01

For example, note the professional approach here:

"Frankenstein" clearly conveys the centrality of the visual to the monstrous. Even the creature is horrified when he encounters his own reflection in a pool and becomes 'fully convinced that I was in reality the monster that I am' (p. 116). In this society, the text suggests, only a blind man, a figure of Blind Justice perhaps, could accept Frankenstein's creature. To a great extent, De Lacey's blindness represents the blindness of the reader. We too do not see the monster and therefore are more concerned with what he says than with how he looks.

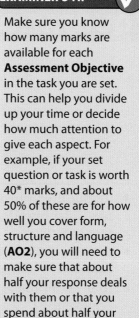

EXAMINER'S TIP

Make sure you know how many marks are available for each **Assessment Objective** in the task you are set. This can help you divide up your time or decide how much attention to give each aspect. For example, if your set question or task is worth 40* marks, and about 50% of these are for how well you cover form, structure and language (**AO2**), you will need to make sure that about half your response deals with them or that you spend about half your time writing about them

This is just an example; check your own specific course for accurate information.

QUESTIONS WITH STATEMENTS, QUOTATIONS OR VIEWPOINTS

One type of question you may come across is one that includes a statement, quotation or viewpoint from another reader.

These questions ask you to respond to, or argue for/against, a specific point of view or critical interpretation.

For *Frankenstein* these questions will typically be like this:

- **'Gothic literature is concerned with the conflicts and anxieties of its particular historical moment.' Discuss with particular reference to** *Frankenstein.*
- **With particular reference to** *Frankenstein,* **discuss the view that Gothic literature is transgressive.**
- **How far do you agree with the idea that Victor is the true monster in** *Frankenstein***?**
- **To what extent do you agree that** *Frankenstein* **demonstrates the importance of sympathy and friendship?**

The key thing to remember is that you are being asked to **respond to a critical interpretation** of the text – in other words, to come up with **your own 'take'** on the idea or viewpoint in the task.

SKILL	MEANS?	HOW DO I ACHIEVE THIS?
Consider different interpretations	There will be more than one way of looking at the given question. For example, critics might be divided about the degree to which **Gothic** is subversive or conservative.	• Show you have considered these different interpretations in your answer. For example: *While it is true that "Frankenstein" is subversive in its attack on social injustice and its demonstration of the need for reform, the text nevertheless also reveals a more conservative fear of revolution and mob violence.*
Write with a clear, personal voice	Your own 'take' on the question is made obvious to the marker. You are not just repeating other people's ideas, but offering what **you** think.	• Although you may mention different perspectives on the task, you settle on your own view. • Use language that shows careful, but confident, consideration. For example: *Although it has been said that … I feel that …*
Construct a coherent argument	The examiner or marker can follow your train of thought so that your own viewpoint is clear to him or her.	• Write in clear paragraphs that deal logically with different aspects of the question. • Support what you say with well-selected and relevant evidence. • Use a range of connectives to help 'signpost' your argument. For example: *There is, however, no happy ending in "Frankenstein". All quests end in failure and the body count is high. Furthermore, the ending is 'open', marked by ambiguity. The monster is 'lost in darkness and distance' (p. 225). Consequently, the reader never sees his death: it remains something always projected in the future, always anticipated but positioned beyond the boundaries of the text.*

ANSWERING A 'VIEWPOINT' QUESTION

Here is an example of a typical question on *Frankenstein*:

> **Robert Kiely argues that 'while the main theme of** *Frankenstein* **is the monstrous consequences of egotism, the counter-theme is the virtue of friendship'. How far do you agree with this statement?**

STAGE 1: DECODE THE QUESTION

Underline/highlight the **key words**, and make sure you understand what the statement, quotation or viewpoint is saying. In this case:

● The key words = **monstrous / egotism / virtue / friendship**
● The viewpoint/idea expressed = *Frankenstein* **attributes all the disastrous events of the novel to Victor's egotism**, i.e. his constant focus on his own self-interests, but it offsets this with the suggestion that this could all have been avoided through friendship/sympathy with and concern for others.
● How far do you agree = **Is Victor egotistical/is he to blame/is friendship the answer?**

STAGE 2: DECIDE WHAT YOUR VIEWPOINT IS

Examiners have stated that they tend to reward a strong view which is clearly put. Think about the question. Can you take issue with it? Disagreeing strongly can lead to higher marks, provided you have **genuine evidence** to support your point of view. Don't disagree just for the sake of it.

STAGE 3: DECIDE HOW TO STRUCTURE YOUR ANSWER

Pick out the key points you wish to make, and decide on the order in which you will present them. Keep this basic plan to hand while you write your response.

STAGE 4: WRITE YOUR RESPONSE

● You could start by expanding on the statement or viewpoint expressed in the question. For example, in **paragraph 1**:

According to Robert Kiely, "Frankenstein" suggests that all the problems stem from Victor's egotism, that is, from Victor's constant focus on his own self-interests; nevertheless, Kiely adds, the text offsets this with the suggestion all could have been avoided through the valuing of friendship, through acting in sympathy with, and out of concern for, others.

This could help by setting up the various ideas you will choose to explore, argue for/against, and so on. But do not just repeat what the question says or just say what you are going to do. Get straight to the point. For example:

However, although there is much evidence in the text to support placing the blame on Victor's egotism, we might argue that it is not quite as simple as this and that, as Elizabeth's failed attempt to plead for Justine most strikingly demonstrates, in a corrupt society friendship and sympathy are perhaps not the powerful forces we might like to believe they should be.

● Then proceed to set out the different arguments or critical perspectives, including your own. This might be done by dealing with specific aspects or elements of the novel one by one. Consider giving 1–2 paragraphs to explore each aspect in turn. Discuss the strengths and weaknesses in each particular point of view. For example:

Paragraph 2: first aspect:

To answer whether the critic's interpretation is valid, we need to **first of all** *look at …*

It is clear from this that …/a **strength** *of this argument is*

However, I believe this suggests that …/a **weakness** *in this argument is*

Paragraph 3: a new focus or aspect:
Turning our attention to the critical idea that … it could be said that …

Paragraphs 4, 5, etc. onwards: develop the argument, building a convincing set of points:

Furthermore, if we look at …

Last paragraph: end with a clear statement of your view, without simply listing all the points you have made.

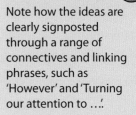

EXAMINER'S TIP

You should comment concisely, professionally and thoughtfully and present a range of viewpoints. Try using modal verbs such as 'could', 'might', 'may' to clarify your own interpretation. For additional help on **Using critical interpretations and perspectives**, see pages 84 and 85

EXAMINER'S TIP

Note how the ideas are clearly signposted through a range of connectives and linking phrases, such as 'However' and 'Turning our attention to …'.

COMPARING *FRANKENSTEIN* WITH OTHER TEXTS

As part of your assessment, you may have to compare *Frankenstein* with or link it to other texts that you have studied. These may be other novels, plays or even poetry. You may also have to link or draw in references from texts written by critics. A typical linking or comparison question might be:

> **Compare the use of the supernatural in *Frankenstein* and another text you have studied.**

THE TASK

Your task is likely to be on a method, issue, viewpoint or key aspect that is common to *Frankenstein* and the other text(s), so you will need to:

> **Evaluate the issue** or statement and have an **open-minded approach**. The best answers suggest meanings and interpretations (plural):
> - Do you agree with the statement? Is this aspect more important in one text than in another? Why? How? How is the supernatural used in these texts?
> - What do I understand by 'supernatural'? Are there any 'real' supernatural beings or the supernatural only used **metaphorically**? Is it the same for both texts?
> - What are the different ways that this question or aspect can be read or viewed?

> **Express original or creative approaches** fluently:
> - This isn't about coming up with entirely new ideas, but you need to show that you're actively engaged with thinking about the question and are not just reeling off things you have learned.
> - **Synthesise** your ideas – pull ideas and points together to create something fresh.
> - This is a linking/comparison response, so ensure that you guide your reader through your ideas logically, clearly and with professional language.

> **Know what to compare/contrast: form, structure** and **language** will **always** be central to your response, even where you also have to write about characters, contexts or culture.
> - Think about: **narrative perspective**, use of flashback, **foreshadowing**, open-ended nature of conclusions.
> - Consider different characteristic uses of language: abstract and concrete language, ambiguity in language, imagistic use of language.
> - Look at a variety of **symbols**, **images**, motifs (how they represent concerns of author/time; what they are and how and where they appear; how they link to critical perspectives; their purposes, effects and impact on the novel).
> - Consider aspects of **genre** (to what extent do the authors of the text conform to/challenge/subvert particular genres or styles of writing?).

WRITING YOUR RESPONSE

The depth and extent of your answer will depend on how much you have to write, but the key will be to **explore in detail**, and **link between ideas and texts**.

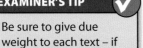
GRADE BOOSTER **A02**

In her 1831 Introduction, Shelley declares her desire to 'curdle the blood, and quicken the beatings of the heart' (p. 8). This is the first of many signals to the reader that *Frankenstein* should be placed in the **genre** of the **Gothic**. The term covers a wide variety of texts and is by no means simple to define, but the genre is generally considered to have emerged in the later eighteenth century as a reaction to – or even a necessary product of – Enlightenment modernity: the **antithesis** to the privileged rationalism of the age.

EXAMINER'S TIP ✓

Be sure to give due weight to each text – if there are two texts, this would normally mean giving them equal attention (but check the exact requirements of your task). Where required or suggested by the course you are following, you could try moving fluently between the texts in each paragraph, as an alternative to treating texts separately. This approach can be impressive and will ensure that comparison is central to your response.

INTRODUCTION TO YOUR RESPONSE

- In relation to the question above, you might begin by briefly outlining what is meant by 'supernatural' in these particular texts: does this mean ghosts, gods or devils? Are you interpreting supernatural literally or metaphorically?

- You could begin with a powerful quotation to launch into your response. For example:

> *'One need not be a chamber to be haunted', the American poet Emily Dickinson wrote in 1862, and by this time such Gothic fictions as Mary Shelley's "Frankenstein" and Emily Brontë's "Wuthering Heights" had already demonstrated precisely this point. By the early nineteenth century, the haunted castle had been replaced by the haunted consciousness: the supernatural is primarily used in a metaphorical sense. Victor is haunted by his creation as Heathcliff is haunted by Catherine, but whether there are any actual supernatural beings in either text is a question open to debate.*

MAIN BODY OF YOUR RESPONSE

- **Point 1:** start with the idea of the supernatural, and what happens to it in the worlds of the novels you are writing about. Is it treated similarly in both? Point out Mary Shelley's claim to be writing a ghost story in her Introduction, and consider why she says this. Then show the way the supernatural is used only metaphorically in *Frankenstein*, to indicate, for example, Victor's guilt, or his internal rage. What does all this imply about the secular world in which the text is produced. What do the critics say? Are there contextual/cultural factors to consider?

- **Point 2:** now cover a new factor or aspect through comparison or contrast of the treatment of the supernatural in another text. Can we be as confident that the supernatural is used only metaphorically in, for example, *Wuthering Heights*? Or do we find the shifting boundaries of reality and dream make this more difficult to decide? How does language contribute to this? What about form and narrative function: for example, do the eminently sensible perspectives of Nelly and Lockwood convince us there are no 'unquiet slumbers' or does the very fact it is these unimaginative people who claim this make us suspect quite the opposite? What do the critics say? Are there contextual/cultural factors to consider?

- **Points 3, 4, 5, etc.:** address a range of new factors and aspects, for example:
  - the way in which boundaries between self and other are set up in the texts
  - the way in which the supernatural, or language of the supernatural, is used to challenge and break down these boundaries – between Victor and monster, Heathcliff and Catherine
  - the different ways you respond to these (with more empathy, greater criticism, less interest?) – and why. For example:

> *One of the more interesting ways in which the supernatural functions in these texts is in either breaking down or reinforcing boundaries of self and other. In "Frankenstein", the language of the supernatural functions to merge Victor and the monster; for example, when Victor describes himself as the only 'unquiet' (p. 94) thing that wanders restless, he becomes the monstrous figure in the scene.*

CONCLUSION

- Synthesise elements of what you have said into a final paragraph that fluently, succinctly and inventively leaves the reader/examiner with the sense that you have engaged with this task and the texts.

> *Ultimately, "Frankenstein" is more definitive in erasing the supernatural from the strikingly secular world of the text. Here it is used purely metaphorically and it functions primarily to break down boundaries, to conflate the creator and his creation. With "Wuthering Heights", we remain on less certain ground. While the supernatural again functions metaphorically, the dead may also return. When they do, they serve only to reinforce the boundaries of self and other and ensure that the desire to merge with the other remains frustrated until the very end.*

GRADE BOOSTER A02

Examiners will be impressed if you demonstrate close attention to the language, particularly when dialogue contributes to characterisation. With Walton, this may involve such observations as his general tendency to speak in the language of the **Romantic** poets, or his repeated use of the term 'brother' in referring to Victor.

EXAMINER'S TIP

Be creative with your conclusion! It's the last thing the examiner will read and your chance to make your mark.

CONTEXT **A04**

Referring to his anticipated departure, Walton quotes from Coleridge's 'The Rime of the Ancient Mariner' (1798) and explains how Coleridge has influenced him: 'there is a love for the marvellous, a belief in the marvellous, intertwined in all my projects, which hurries me out of the common pathways of men' (p. 22). Here Walton reveals the influence of **Romanticism** on his personality and sets the stage for the appearance of Frankenstein on his sledge. Victor, like the ancient mariner, will have a marvellous tale to tell.

EXAMINER'S TIP ✓

You may be asked to discuss other texts you have studied as well as *Frankenstein* as part of your response. Once you have completed your response on the novel you could move on to discuss the same issues in your other texts. Begin with a simple linking phrase or sentence to launch straight into your first point about your next text, such as: *The title of Emily Brontë's "Wuthering Heights" might suggest that here too there will be an emphasis on wild and desolate landscapes, but Brontë actually makes more symbolic use of the house, with the divisions and boundaries of its rooms and enclosures, than of the wide open spaces of the surrounding moors.*

RESPONDING TO A GENERAL QUESTION ABOUT THE WHOLE TEXT

You may also be asked to write about a specific aspect of *Frankenstein* – but as it relates to the whole text. For example:

> **Explore the symbolic use of the settings in *Frankenstein*.**

This means you should:

- Decide which aspects of the settings to discuss.
- Explain their **symbolic** functions: how they are used in terms of developing character for example, **foreshadowing** action, or developing themes. Look carefully at the language used to describe the settings.
- Look at aspects of the **whole novel**, not just one part of it.

STRUCTURING YOUR RESPONSE

You need a clear, logical plan, as for all tasks that you do.

It is impossible to write about every section or part of the text, so you will need to:

- Quickly note 5–6 key points or aspects to build your essay around

  Point a *Alps and glaciers: healing and restorative nature*

  Point b *Alps and glaciers: threatening, alien nature*

  Point c *The Arctic: Walton's illusions of tropical paradise vs cold, ice, threatening space, suggests death. In terms of structure it surrounds the novel*

  Point d *Orkneys: desolate natural setting for the making of the female creature as opposed to civilised city for the making of the male creature*

  Point e *Weather: how it changes the landscape, suggests inner rage, foreshadows arrival of monster and contributes to sense of duality*

- Decide the most effective or logical order. For example, point **c**, then **b**, **a**, **d**, and **e**.

You could begin with your key or main idea, with supporting evidence/references, followed by your further points (perhaps two paragraphs for each). For example: …

Paragraph 1: first key point. *While some of the events in 'Frankenstein' take place within cities, we learn little about these settings, and the emphasis is rather upon wilder and less civilised worlds. The icy Arctic landscape that surrounds 'Frankenstein' – it is, after all, when the narrative both begins and ends – is a barren and sterile world …*

Paragraph 2: expand out, link areas. *The Arctic connects to the Swiss Alps, with their 'white and shining pyramids' (p. 97) of snow and more particularly to the glacier, Mer de Glace (sea of ice) …*

Paragraph 3: change direction, introduce new aspect/point. *This view of the Alps as a desolate and sterile world is at odds, however, with the view of the Alps as part of a healing and restorative nature that is sometimes found in Victor's descriptions …*

And so on.

- For your **conclusion**, use a compelling way to finish, perhaps repeating some or all of the key words from the question. For example, either:

End with your final point, but **add a last clause** which makes it clear what you think is key to the answer:

No matter which aspect of the landscape we examine, what is important is not so much what it is, but how it is perceived by the observing character.

Or end with a **new quotation** or an **aspect** that's **slightly different** from your main point.

The sunny tropical paradise that Walton once envisioned then, that 'region of beauty and delight' (p. 15), remains a dream … Or, of course, you can **combine** these endings.

WRITING ABOUT CONTEXTS

Assessment Objective 4 asks you to 'demonstrate understanding of the significance and influence of the contexts in which literary texts are written and received ...'. This can mean:

- How the events, settings, politics and so on **of the time when the text was written** influenced the writer or help us to understand the novel's themes or concerns. For example, how was Shelley influenced by contemporary debates over the life-principle?

or

- How events, settings, politics and so on **of the time when the text is read or seen** influence how it is understood. For example, would readers familiar with contemporary debates about cloning or genetic foods be more inclined to see *Frankenstein* as a warning of the potentially negative consequences of developments in science and technology?

THE CONTEXT FOR *FRANKENSTEIN*

You might find the following table helpful for thinking about how particular aspects of the time contribute to our understanding of the novel and its themes. These are just examples – can you think of any others?

POLITICAL	LITERARY	PHILOSOPHICAL
French Revolution	**Romanticism** – imagination and nature	Burke and the **sublime**
Class conflict and the Pentridge uprising	**Gothic** – horror and terror	Educational theories of Locke and Rousseau

SCIENTIFIC	CULTURAL	SOCIAL
Electricity and galvanism Life-principle Arctic exploration	Enlightenment Rationalism Rejection of superstition	Education and rights of women The bourgeois family

TARGETING A HIGH GRADE   **A04**

Remember that the extent to which you write about these contexts will be determined by the marks available. Some questions or tasks may have very few marks allocated for **AO4**, but where you do have to refer to context the key thing is **not** to 'bolt on' your comments, or write a separate chunk of text on context and then 'go back' to the novel. For example:

Don't just write:

By 1814, a debate over what came to be known as the 'life-principle' had caused a rift in the sciences, represented by the differing positions of John Abernethy and William Lawrence. Lawrence advocated a purely materialist position while Abernethy argued for the presence of some metaphysical vital principle that might be linked to the idea of the soul. Shelley was obviously aware of these debates ...

Do write:

The question that preoccupies Victor Frankenstein, 'Whence ... did the principle of life proceed?' (p. 52), was a matter of intense debate during the years in which "Frankenstein" was conceived and written, and a debate with which Shelley was demonstrably familiar. She creates an eminently secular world, no gods, no spirits, suggesting she leans towards the purely materialist position in the debate rather than agreeing with those who argued for the presence of some vital principle that might be linked to the soul.

CONTEXT   **A04**

The Romantic movement is usually considered to originate around 1789, the year of the French Revolution, which, like the American Revolution, was optimistically seen by Godwin, Wordsworth and others as the beginnings of a new age of justice and equality for all. It was a time of social unrest and political activism, even in England.

USING CRITICAL INTERPRETATIONS AND PERSPECTIVES

THE 'MEANING' OF A TEXT

There are many viewpoints and perspectives on the 'meaning' of *Frankenstein*, and examiners will be looking for evidence that you have considered a range of these. Broadly speaking, these different interpretations might relate to:

1. CHARACTER

- Is the character an 'archetype' (a specific type of character with common features)? Victor Frankenstein can, for example, be considered the archetype of the 'overreacher', someone who aims for something beyond normal human reach, a type associated with such other characters as Prometheus or Doctor Faustus.
- Does the character personify, **symbolise** or represent a specific idea or trope? Is Victor an example of the psychologically tormented, a man with a radically split psyche? Does he demonstrate the ways in which egotism and ambition become destructive?
- Is the character modern, universal, of his/her time, historically accurate, etc.? For example, how is Victor Frankenstein related to or distinct from 'mad scientists' of the Victorian age or of the present age?

2. IDEAS AND ISSUES

- The monstrous and the human
- Egotism and benevolence
- Nature and the sublime
- Social injustice

3. LINKS TO OTHER TEXTS AND IDEAS

- What is the novel's influence culturally, historically and socially? Do we see echoes of the characters or genres in other texts? How does the text rewrite Milton's *Paradise Lost* for a secular age? How does the idea of Frankenstein's creature look back to such monstrous figures as the golem, and forward to such figures as the replicants of Ridley Scott's *Blade Runner*? (To see one particularly interesting connection, watch the 'Tears in the Rain' speech from *Blade Runner*, and compare this with the monster's final speech to Walton.)
- How does its language link to other texts or modes, such as other **Gothic** texts, **Romantic** poetry, classical and Christian myths and legends?

4. DRAMATIC STRUCTURE

- Does the novel follow any **conventions** peculiar to Gothic fictions?
- What is the function of setting, characters, **imagery**, etc. in relation to narrative?
- How are the **narratives embedded** and why? What are the specific moments of tension, conflict, crisis and denouement – and do we agree on what they are?

5. AUDIENCE RESPONSE

- How does Shelley **position** the reader? Are we to empathise with, feel distance from, judge and/or evaluate the events and characters?

CONTEXT **A04**

Today we often use the term 'Frankenstein science' to describe developments in which scientists appear to be overreaching themselves, including, for example, experiments with cloning.

---

6. CRITICAL REACTION

- How do different readers view the novel: for example, in Victorian, postwar or more recent times; feminist critics as opposed to psychoanalytical or structuralist critics?

WRITING ABOUT CRITICAL PERSPECTIVES

The important thing to remember is that **you** are a critic too. Your job is to evaluate what a critic or school of criticism has said about the elements above, and arrive at your own conclusions. In essence, you need to: **consider** the views of others, **synthesise** them, then decide on **your perspective**. For example:

EXPLAIN THE VIEWPOINTS

Critical view A about the creation of the monster:

> *The earliest critical readings of "Frankenstein" often saw Victor's primary transgression as being against God; that is, he usurps the power of God in creating a being.*

Critical view B about the creation of the monster:

> *Feminist readings of the late 1970s and 1980s began to rethink the novel by pointing out that Victor Frankenstein usurps not the power of God but the reproductive power of women.*

THEN SYNTHESISE AND ADD YOUR PERSPECTIVE

Synthesise these views whilst adding your own:

> *The idea put forward by early critics that Victor's primary transgression was against God is to a certain extent supported by Shelley herself in her Introduction. However, this Introduction was added many years after the novel was first published, and there is little support for such an argument in the actual text: this constructs a very secular world where there are no gods to offend. Feminist critics of the late 1970s and 1980s alternately argued that Victor's main crime is not to usurp the power of God, but the reproductive power of women. I would argue, however, that there is much more evidence in the text to suggest Victor's main crime is not what he does, but what he fails to do: he does not nurture the being he creates; he does not fulfil his obligations towards his 'child'.*

TARGETING A HIGH GRADE   A03

Make sure you have thoroughly explored the different types of criticism written about *Frankenstein*. Critical interpretation of novels can range from reviews and comments written about the text at the time that it was first published through to critical analysis by a modern critic or reader writing today. Bear in mind that views of texts can change over time as values and experiences themselves change, and that criticism can be written for different purposes. Here are just two examples of different kinds of responses to *Frankenstein*:

Critic 1 – Fred Botting in 'Frankenstein, Werther and the Monster of Love' in T. Pinkney, K. Hanley and Fred Botting, *Romanticism, Theory, Gender* (1995): 'The mother occupies a central place in Frankenstein's world. Idealised, her loss forms the site on which Frankenstein's desires take their particular form: to conquer death is to overcome her death and recuperate her, while to "give birth" to life is both to fulfil her desire for a daughter and to occupy the place of the mother' (p. 173).

Critic 2 – Dale Townshend in *The Orders of Gothic* (2007): 'It is nothing new to say that mothers in *Frankenstein* are strikingly absent, and not only most obviously or in relation to the monster itself' (p. 139).

CHECK THE FILM   A04

Ken Russell's *Gothic* (1986) and Ivan Passer's *Haunted Summer* (1988) are both loosely based on the events of the summer of 1816.

ANNOTATED SAMPLE ANSWERS

Below are extracts from two sample answers to the same question at different grades. Bear in mind that these are examples only, covering all four Assessment Objectives – you will need to check the type of question and the weightings given for the four AOs when writing your coursework essay or practising for your exam.

> Question: **Some readers have commented that Mary Shelley presents the monster as more human than his creator. How far do you agree with this view?**

CANDIDATE 1

AO4 While this is potentially useful context, you don't directly mention the idea of the 'human'. The idea in the opening could also have been condensed and offered in a sentence or two.

AO1 'could be said' by whom? Notice the question says specifically that it is often claimed 'Mary Shelley presents the monster as more human …'. What would she have thought of as human? Read the question more carefully and think about key terms.

Mary Shelley's "Frankenstein" was written when there was a lot of debate over the question of the life principle. John Abernethy, President of the Royal College of Surgeons, and his pupil William Lawrence, appointed as second Professor at the College in 1815 had different opinions. Lawrence looked at life from a very materialist position. Abernethy wanted to keep something in common with religious beliefs and argued that life could not be explained in material terms; something else was required that might be linked to the concept of the immortal soul. It's within this context that Mary Shelley makes Victor Frankenstein create a monster that could be said to be more human than he is.

AO1 Don't use contractions in a formal essay.

AO3 Strong personal expression but the argument is not completely clear.

I think it would be difficult to argue for the creature's humanity if human means the species. He's constructed out of a mixture of dead parts taken from graveyards, dissecting rooms and slaughterhouses; he's unnaturally large and demonstrates superhuman speed and abilities. In this respect, he is not human, but, as Victor initially planned, one of a 'new species'.

On the basis of his appearance, those who see him call him monstrous and not human. By calling the monster the 'filthy mass that moved and talked', for example, Victor denies his humanity, and makes him into a monstrous thing 'too horrible for human eyes to behold'. Victor wants always to name and blame 'the filthy daemon' (p. 77), the 'devil' (p. 78), the 'animal' (p. 79) and to decide that the monster's 'delight was in carnage and misery' (p. 78). This is how humans create monsters. Victor uses words to define the monster as other, to divide the human from the demonic or animalistic.

AO2 This is excellent close reading and good attention to the language, and Shelley does indeed show how humans creates monsters. But is this really the question you have been asked to address?

AO1 This is turning into a more general discussion on the monstrous and the human. Focus is being lost.

Traditionally, an 'abnormal' appearance would mean the opposite of a 'normal' human. To some extent, Mary Shelley draws upon this tradition in "Frankenstein" with the creation of a monstrous being that no one can look upon without abhorrence. Shelley also, however, challenges this tradition by suggesting true monstrosity is something that emerges more in what we do than in how we look. The monstrous and the human then become less easy to separate and it becomes possible to argue that the being that is called the monster is in fact more human than his monstrous creator.

This is shown in the way the creature longs for friends. He tries to join in with others and they are frightened and reject him. Even the De Lacey family who are seen as very kind and take in Safie won't accept him. His desire for companions, and particularly a female, contrasts with Victor Frankenstein's rejection of family and his evident reluctance to marry Elizabeth. When he talks of their forthcoming 'union' he is talking in very formal terms unlike those we expect from a lover.

A02 This is a crucial point which distinguishes the monster as human from Victor as inhuman, but you need to give more specifics to back up the general points. Analyse the language more.

A02 This is quite a good point to bring in at the end and the quotation from Elizabeth is good. Nevertheless, still more focus on the monster than the human.

It is only when he suffers from the viciousness of human society that he himself begins to act violently, to be a real monster. Shelley shows human beings both create and become monsters. Then again, given the way humans behave in this book, we might also say that his new 'monstrous' behaviour is quite generally characteristic of the 'human'. When Justine is executed that causes Elizabeth to say how, in their violence and cruelty, people appear to be 'monsters thirsting for each other's blood'. If the monster is often human, then the human is often monstrous.

GRADE C

Comment
While this answer shows a good grasp of the text and many of the issues, it is not focused enough on the question and the argument is not constructed in as cohesive a way as it could be (AO1). Aim for more signposts to the reader and a clearer, more formal style. More attention to language and questions of form are also needed (AO2), and for a higher grade, reference to relevant context (AO4) and discussion of alternative critical interpretations are key (AO3).

For a B grade
- The argument needs to be much more focused on the specific question. It gets too generally caught up in questions of human and monstrous.

- There should be more close detailed analysis of language, form and structure.

- Make sure context is relevant to the text.

- Choose a few more useful quotations.

- Mention a critic's perspective.

CANDIDATE 2

Describing his dream of harmoniously living with a female companion in a state of nature, the monster in Mary Shelley's "Frankenstein" says to his creator: 'The picture I present to you is peaceful and human' (p. 149). But what does it mean to be human? In order to argue, as some readers have done, that Mary Shelley is presenting the monster as more human than his creator, it is first necessary to define what Shelley means by the term. After all, as Joanna Bourke demonstrates in 'What it Means to be Human' (2011), the meaning of 'human' is by no means self-evident and often changes throughout history.

> **AO2** Good quotation to start essay and lead into topic.

> **AO1** Engages with question.

> **AO3** Relevant reference to critic.

> **AO1** Recognition of the need to define terms.

For Mary Shelley, I would argue, to be human above all involves sympathetic engagement with others, and in this respect she agrees with her father, William Godwin, that the natural human emotions were those of affection, pity, and, above all, benevolence, a public form of sympathy in the eighteenth century. The text begins with the meeting of two characters, Robert Walton and Victor Frankenstein, who lack such virtues and are characterised by egotism and self-interest. Their deficiencies as humans are symbolically shown in the sterile icy wastes of the Arctic where they meet. This is a desolate Gothic space of terrifying 'mountains of ice', an inhuman landscape which comes to represent emotional as well as physical coldness.

> **AO1** Clear statement of your position on questions of definition.

> **AO4** Good range of contextual references.

> **AO2** Engagement with symbolic values of setting.

This frame narrative sets the context for the very different responses of the creature in his embedded narrative at the very heart of the text. In contrast to Walton and Frankenstein, benevolence, affection and pity are all qualities the creature immediately and apparently instinctively demonstrates, even if he is as yet unable to name the 'sensations of a peculiar and overpowering nature' that he experiences. His instinctual benevolence is shown in his saving the young girl from drowning and in his various attempts to help the De Lacey family, cutting their wood, doing their chores. He longs for companionship, to be accepted with the 'kindness and affection' he observes demonstrated in the De Lacey family. His desire for companionship, and more specifically for a mate, contrasts strikingly with Victor Frankenstein's rejection of family and his evident reluctance to settle what he repeatedly describes, with what we might suspect is a shudder, as his 'union' with Elizabeth. There is little 'affection' implied in this very formal term.

> **AO2** Structure and its function considered.

> **AO2** Analysis of 'human' through contrast.

> **AO2** Helpful analysis of language.

If Shelley is, as I have suggested, equating the human with the qualities of benevolence, pity and sympathy, then we must concede that the creature loses his humanity and does become truly monstrous once he becomes obsessed with revenge. Denied the sympathies for which he longs, the creature, he himself admits, becomes miserable, and misery makes him 'a fiend', destroying what he cannot

> **AO3** Moving to an alternative position.

AO1 Use of literary terms.

have. At this moment, allusions to "Paradise Lost" confirm a fall from the human: the monster stops seeing himself in human terms as a new Adam and begins to associate himself rather with the 'fiend' who has 'cast off all feeling'. 'Evil', he adds, quoting Milton's Satan, 'thenceforth became my good'. While nothing excuses the way the creature has been treated, as Anne McWhir reminds us, he does have choices and perhaps does not make the right ones.

Reference to other literary texts. **AO3**

AO3 Critical viewpoint.

It is at this moment too, if we move to a psychological reading of the text, that the creature begins to act as Victor's dark double or doppelganger. Destroying what he cannot have, the creature acts out Victor's rejection of relationships that bind him to family and community, his rejection of familial and sexual love, all things that might interfere with the pursuit of his own needs and desires. The creature, then, loses his humanity as he merges with, and acts for, his creator.

Use of concepts. **AO1**

AO1 Use of connectives to produce cohesive argument.

We can, therefore, see the monster's nature as essentially human but twisted by his misery. Additionally, we can see the monster's humanity eroded by his function as the dark double enacting Victor's own rejection of human sympathies and the obligations they entail. These two readings might, finally, come together to explain one of the more puzzling aspects of the novel's conclusion. This is the moment when Walton finds him hanging over Victor's coffin, full of 'grief and horror' at what he has done.

Walton's response - and we might pause to consider how unreliable his perspective has been throughout - is to dismiss the creature's remorse, his coming 'to whine over the desolation' that he has made. He called the monster a hypocrite. There may, however, be more to it than this, particularly since this looks back quite explicitly to the portrait of Caroline Beaufort, epitome of benevolence, sympathy and pity, painted in an 'agony of despair' over the coffin of her father. It may well be that with Victor's death, the creature's function as dark double is over, giving another reading to his comment that 'He is dead who called me into being'. And it may well be that while driven to monstrous behaviour by the treatment he receives from all, the creature until the very end retains some remnants of sympathy and affection, those qualities which Mary Shelley suggests are the very essence of what makes us human.

Good narrative link. **AO2**

AO3 Pushing the analysis deeper by noticing possible alternative meanings.

AO1 Conveys a sense that you are reaching your conclusion and returns us to the main question and also to Shelley's idea of the human.

GRADE A

Comment
There is an excellent focus on the question here, and what is particularly impressive is the way that the question has been thought about carefully and the terms of the question considered (AO1). It is generally well written, and there is some good analysis of language and some excellent narrative links are made (AO2). There is intelligent use of critical viewpoints and theory (AO3) and relevant context (AO4).

For an A* grade
- Aim for a little more detailed analysis of language.
- A little more specific context on 'benevolence' could be added, but don't get sidetracked from the focus.

WORKING THROUGH A TASK

Now it's your turn to work through a task on *Frankenstein*. The key is to:

- Read/decode the task/question.
- Plan your points – then expand and link your points.
- Draft your answer.

TASK TITLE

'Remorse is the dominant feeling expressed by the monster in the final chapter of *Frankenstein*.' Do you agree with this statement or do you think that remorse is tempered by continuing anger and bitterness?

DECODE THE QUESTION: KEY WORDS

Do you agree… = what are your views and upon what evidence do you base them?

Remorse = sorrow and regret for past deeds

Dominant feeling = the main sentiment expressed

PLAN AND EXPAND

- Key aspect: evidence of remorse

POINT	POINT EXPANDED	QUOTATIONS
Point a *Remorse shown in actions*	• *Monster found hanging over the coffin of Frankenstein* • *Jones notes how this looks back to the portrait of Caroline Beaufort and dead father.* • *Hand outstretched takes us back to moment after his 'birth' when he reaches out to 'father'*	Quotations 1–2 • *'Caroline Beaufort in an agony of despair, kneeling by the coffin of her dead father' (p. 79)* • *'one hand was stretched out' (p. 59) / 'one vast hand was extended' (p. 221)*
Point b *Remorse shown in what he says*	Different aspects of this point expanded *You fill in*	Quotations 1–2 *You fill in*
Point c *Decision to destroy himself*	Different aspects of this point expanded *You fill in*	Quotations 1–2 *You fill in*

- Key aspect: evidence of anger and bitterness

POINT	POINT EXPANDED	QUOTATIONS
Point a *You fill in*	Different aspects of this point expanded *You fill in*	Quotations 1–2 *You fill in*
Point b *You fill in*	Different aspects of this point expanded *You fill in*	Quotations 1–2 *You fill in*
Point c *You fill in*	Different aspects of this point expanded *You fill in*	Quotations 1–2 *You fill in*

CONCLUSION

POINT	POINT EXPANDED	QUOTATIONS
Key final point or overall view *You fill in*	Draw together and perhaps add a final further point to support your view *You fill in*	Final quotation to support your view *You fill in*

DEVELOP FURTHER AND DRAFT

Now look back over your draft points and:

- Add further links or connections between the points to develop them further or synthesise what has been said, for example:

> *However, while he professes to hate himself for driving his creator to death, it is clear from the final paragraphs that he continues to wallow in self-pity, never really taking responsibility for his actions. My agony, he proclaims, 'was still superior to thine' (p. 225).*

- Decide an order for your points/paragraphs – some may now be linked/connected and therefore **not** in the order of the table above.

Now draft your essay. If you're really stuck you can use the opening paragraph below to get you started.

> *The one word that dominates the dialogue between Walton and the monster in the final chapter of "Frankenstein" is 'remorse'. Walton is not immediately convinced by his sincerity: 'Wretch!', he exclaims, 'it is well that you come here to whine over the desolation that you have made … Hypocritical fiend!' (p. 223). We may well be equally suspicious over the monster's self-reproaches. While on the one hand he expresses remorse both through what he says and what he does, on the other hand he continues to rage against the injustice done to him and to be more concerned with his own miseries than with those he has inflicted upon others.*

Once you've written your essay, turn to page 96 for a mark scheme on this question to see how well you've done.

FURTHER QUESTIONS

1) 'I bore a hell within me', says Victor Frankenstein. To what extent does Shelley show that true horror lies within?
2) Gothic spaces reflect states of mind. To what extent is this true in *Frankenstein*?
3) To what extent do you agree that Victor Frankenstein's crime is to usurp the procreative powers of women?
4) '*Frankenstein*, with its descriptions of bodily decay, demonstrates the growing antipathy towards death during the later eighteenth and nineteenth centuries.' What evidence do you find for such a position?
5) '*Frankenstein* is a text full of mirroring and duplication.' How far do you agree with this statement?
6) The monster claims 'he is malicious because he is miserable'. To what extent do you agree with his assessment in the light of two or more texts you have studied?
7) 'Gothic literature engages with the anxieties of the age that produces it.' Discuss some of the major themes of the works you have read in light of this comment.
8) 'The supernatural is central to the Gothic'. How far do you agree with this statement in the light of two or more texts you have studied?
9) 'While Gothic fictions change, many motifs recur with remarkable persistence.' To what extent can you find support for this position in *Frankenstein* and at least one other text?
10) 'Dreams reveal the inner horrors of Gothic fictions.' Consider the function of dreams in *Frankenstein* in light of this statement.

ESSENTIAL STUDY TOOLS

FURTHER READING

ON FRANKENSTEIN

Chris Baldick, *In Frankenstein's Shadow: Myth, Monstrosity and Nineteenth-century Writing*, Oxford University Press, 1990

The monster as mythic image in nineteenth-century literature

Jonathan Bate, *The Song of the Earth*, Harvard University Press, 2000

Seminal work of eco-criticism with brief discussion of *Frankenstein*

Fred Botting, *Making Monstrous: Frankenstein, Criticism, Theory*, Manchester University Press, 1991

Challenging poststructuralist analysis for the advanced reader

—— ed., *Frankenstein*, Macmillan, 1995

A useful collection of some of the most significant essays written on *Frankenstein*; the novel is examined from a wide variety of theoretical perspectives

Peter Brooks, '"Godlike Science/Unhallowed Arts": Language, Nature, and Monstrosity', in Levine and Knoepflmacher, eds., *The Endurance of Frankenstein*, pp. 205–20

A useful discussion of language in *Frankenstein*

Kate Ellis, 'Monsters in the Garden: Mary Shelley and the Bourgeois Family', in Levine and Knoepflmacher, eds., *The Endurance of Frankenstein*, pp. 123–42

Reads Victor's rebellion as a rebellion against the family

George Levine and U. C. Knoepflmacher, eds., *The Endurance of Frankenstein: Essays on Mary Shelley's Novel*, University of California Press, 1979

Useful collection of essays that changed the course of *Frankenstein* criticism – a good place to start further research

Anne McWhir, 'Teaching the Monster to Read', in John Willinksy, ed., *The Educational Legacy of Romanticism*, Wilfrid Laurier University Press, 1990, pp. 73–92

Frankenstein in the context of educational theories

Ellen Moers, 'Female Gothic', in Levine and Knoepflmacher, eds., *The Endurance of Frankenstein*, pp. 77–87

Reads *Frankenstein* as a birth myth

Bill Phillips, 'Frankenstein and Shelley's "Wet Ungenial Summer"', Atlantis, 28.2, 2005, pp. 59–68

Eco-critical discussion of climate and environment in the text

Joyce Zonana, 'They Will Prove the Truth of My Tale', *Journal of Narrative Technique*, 21.2, 1991, pp. 170–84

Feminist reading focusing on Safie's letters

ON SHELLEY'S LIFE AND OTHER WORKS

Anne Mellor, *Mary Shelley: Her Life, Her Fiction, Her Monsters*, Routledge, 1988

Excellent for both biographical information and a clear analysis of the whole range of Shelley's work

HISTORICAL CONTEXT

Philippe Ariès, *The Hour of Our Death*, trans. Helen Weaver, Knopf, 1981

An historical analysis of attitudes towards death

Susan E. Lederer, *Frankenstein: Penetrating the Secrets of Nature*, Rutgers University Press, 2002

Interesting focus on science and technology

Tim Marshall, *Murdering to Dissect: Grave-robbing, Frankenstein and the Anatomy Literature*, Manchester University Press, 1995

Literary historical approach

LITERARY CONTEXT

Sue Chaplin, *Gothic Literature: Texts, Contexts, Connections*, York Press, 2011

Excellent introduction and highly accessible

Claire Kahane, 'The Gothic Mirror', in Claire Kahane and Medelon Sprengnether, eds., *The (M)other Tongue: Essays in Feminist Psychoanalytic Interpretation*, Cornell University Press, 1985, pp. 334–51

Classic essay on the Gothic from psychoanalytical perspective focusing on the heroine

Robert Kiely, *The Romantic Novel in England*, Harvard University Press, 1972

Generic study

David Lodge, *The Art of Fiction*, Viking, 2003

Explores the various methods and techniques used by writers

David Punter and Glennis Byron, eds., *The Gothic*, Blackwell, 2003

Includes material on background, context, key writings and common themes and topics

Dale Townshend, *The Orders of Gothic*, AMS Press, 2007

Advanced theoretical discussion with chapter on *Frankenstein*

LITERARY TERMS

allusion a reference, often only indirect, to another text, person, event, etc.

ambiguity when something can be interpreted in more than one way, often used to suggest uncertainty in meaning

ambivalence simultaneous existence of two different attitudes towards one idea, event, person, etc.

analogy illustration of an idea by means of a more familiar idea that is similar or parallel to it in some way

antithesis a contrast or opposition

atmosphere mood or emotional tone created in a text

closure ending, the process of ending

convention established practice or conspicuous feature which occurs repeatedly in a particular kind of work

double or **doppelgänger** an alter-ego

eco-criticism the study of literature and the environment from an interdisciplinary perspective

epigraph quotation or phrase placed at start of a book

epistolary written in the form of a series of letters

epithet a word or phrase used to define a characteristic quality of a person

eponymous relating to or being the person or thing after which something is named; Frankenstein is the eponymous **protagonist** of Shelley's novel

foreshadowing the strategy by which a text hints at plot developments that will come later in a story

genre a kind; literary type or style

Gothic emerging in the eighteenth century in opposition to the Enlightenment championing of the powers of reason, the privileging of science and rejection of superstition, it focused upon the irrational and the supernatural, on all that the individual and society attempted to suppress in the name of psychic and social stability

imagery use of language to evoke sense-impressions

intertextuality the way a text borrows from and transforms other texts

irony involves a sharp discrepancy between what is said or done and what is meant

juxtaposition the placement of two objects or abstract concepts next to each other, usually in order to achieve particular effects through comparison or contrast

melodrama sensational drama, emotionally exaggerated

metaphor one thing is described in terms of its resemblance to another

narratee the imagined person within the text whom the narrator addresses

narrative perspective or **point of view** the way in which the narrator sees or interprets; **embedded narrative** is a story enclosed within a **frame narrative**, a tale within a tale; **linear narrative** moves chronologically from beginning to end

narrator the person, as distinct from the author, who is telling the story; a **first-person narrator** is presented as an 'I' who is involved in or witness to the events described; a **third-person narrator** is outside the story and refers to all characters as 'he' or 'she'; within the third-person point of view can be distinguished the **omniscient narrator** who seems to know everything about the characters and events and has access to the minds of all, and the **limited narrator** who knows only what is thought and experienced by one character who is defined as the centre of consciousness

noble savage an idea developed by French philosopher Jean-Jacques Rousseau that man in primitive society is more noble than modern urban man, corrupted by civilisation

Oedipal complex the repressed but continuing desire in the male adult to possess the mother and destroy the father; Freud drew the term from the tragedy of Oedipus

'other' otherness means difference, but in continental philosophy, defining the 'other' is part of what constructs the 'self'; Victor constructs himself as rational and civilised in opposition to the creature whom he defines as an irrational and primitive 'other'

oxymoron combination of contradictory words

paradox an apparently contradictory statement which is nevertheless somehow meaningful

parallelism arrangement of similar words or presentation of characters to suggest correspondences between them

parody imitation of another work, often in order to make it amusing or ridiculous

pathetic fallacy the treatment of inanimate objects as though they have human feelings and sensations

pathos involves the depiction of a person or event in a way that appeals to the audience or reader's emotions and sympathies

postmodernism a new way of approaching traditional ideas and practices; postmodern literature reacts to modernism and is frequently playful, self-conscious about its fictional strategies, tending to question the possibility of stable meaning and to undercut distinctions between high and low culture

protagonist leading character in a story

rhetoric the deliberate exploitation of eloquence for persuasive effect

Romanticism an artistic, literary and philosophical movement that originated in the later eighteenth century in Europe, it prized intuition and emotion over Enlightenment rationalism, valued nature and the powers of the imagination and elevated the heroic individual

satire a form in which follies and abuses are held up to ridicule with the hope of leading to improvement – social criticism which uses wit as a weapon

sensibility originally formulated in the eighteenth century as a positive and moral force of compassion and sympathy, it soon degenerated into something of a cult, and the display of exquisite emotion became valued in itself; Walton's ship's master is a man of sensibility in the best sense of the term

simile one thing is likened to another through the use of 'like' or 'as'

slasher a slasher film usually involves a psychopathic killer stalking a group of victims who are killed in a particularly violent manner; John Carpenter's *Halloween* (1987) and Sean S. Cunningham's *Friday the 13th* (1980) are two notable early examples

sublime quality of awesome grandeur, as distinguished from the beautiful, in nature

symbol something representing something else, often an idea or quality, by analogy or association

tone language to suggest mood or atmosphere

tragic hero the protagonist of a tragedy; Aristotle's *Poetics* (*c*. 335 BCE) offered an early definition of a tragic hero – a man who is good, but not too good; his fall is brought about by some error or frailty and evokes pity and fear in the audience

voice mode of expression, used to suggest differences in tone and style

TIMELINE

WORLD EVENTS	SHELLEY'S LIFE	LITERARY EVENTS
		1667 John Milton, *Paradise Lost*
		1750 Jean-Jacques Rousseau expounds idea of 'noble savage'
1752 Benjamin Franklin invents lightning conductor		
	1756 Father, William Godwin, born	
	1759 Mother, Mary Wollstonecraft, born	
		1762 Rousseau's *Emile* suggests child ideally be allowed full scope for development away from harmful influences of civilisation
		1772 Johann Wolfgang von Goethe, *The Sorrows of Young Werther*
1783 American independence recognised		
		1787 Mary Wollstonecraft, *Thoughts on the Education of Daughters*
1789 French Revolution begins		
1790 Luigi Galvani 'discovers' electricity in animal and human limbs		
		1791 Constantin Volney, *Ruins of Empire[s]* published
	1792 Mother goes to Paris with Gilbert Imla	**1792** Mary Wollstonecraft, *A Vindication of the Rights of Woman*
1793 Louis XVI beheaded		**1793** William Godwin, *An Enquiry Concerning Political Justice*
1794 Erasmus Darwin's *Zoonomia* discusses spontaneous generation	**1794** Mother has illegitimate daughter, Fanny	**1794** Godwin, *Caleb Williams*; Thomas Paine, *The Age of Reason*; William Blake, *The Book of Urizen*
		1795 Marquis de Sade, *Philosophie dans le Boudoir*
		1796 Wollstonecraft, *Letters written during a Short Residence in Sweden, Norway and Denmark*
	1797 Mother and father marry; Mary born; mother dies ten days later	
		1798 Samuel Taylor Coleridge, 'The Rime of the Ancient Mariner'
1800 Alessandro Volta creates prototype electric battery		**1800** Maria Edgeworth, *Castle Rackrent*
	1801 Father remarries	
1803 Britain at war with France		
1804 Napoleon becomes emperor		
1805 Battle of Trafalgar		
1806 William Pitt dies		
1807 Slave trade abolished in the British Empire		
		1808 Goethe, *Faust* (Part 1)
1811 Luddite riots		**1811** Jane Austen, *Sense and Sensibility*; Percy Bysshe Shelley, *The Necessity of Atheism*
1812 Napoleon retreats from Moscow		
		1813 Austen, *Pride and Prejudice*
	1814 Mary begins affair with Percy Bysshe Shelley; they elope to Continent	**1814** Percy Bysshe Shelley, *A Refutation of Deism*
	1815 Mary gives birth prematurely to daughter, who dies a few days later	
1816 First wooden stethoscope	**1816** Mary gives birth to son William; Mary and Shelley leave for Geneva; Shelley's wife Harriet drowns; Mary and Shelley marry	**1816** Austen, *Emma*
	1817 Mary writing *Frankenstein*; gives birth to daughter Clara	**1817** Lord Byron, *Manfred*
1818 First (unsuccessful) blood transfusions at Guy's Hospital, London	**1818** *Frankenstein* published; family leave for Italy; daughter Clara dies in Venice	**1818** Percy Bysshe Shelley writes *Prometheus Unbound* (publ. 1820); Thomas Love Peacock, *Nightmare Abbey*; Walter Scott, *Tales of My Landlord*
	1819 Son William dies; Mary writes *Mathilda*, a semi-autobiographical tale of incest; son Percy born	
1820 George III dies		
1821 Napoleon dies	**1821** Mary writes *Valpurga*	
	1822 Percy Bysshe Shelley drowns at sea	
1824 Lord Byron dies	**1824** Mary begins work on *The Last Man*	
1827 Beethoven dies		
	1830 Mary publishes *Perkin Warbeck*	
	1831 Revised edition of *Frankenstein*	
		1832 Goethe, *Faust* (Part 2)
	1835 Mary publishes *Lodore*	
	1836 Mary's father dies	
	1837 Mary's *Falkner* published	
	1851 Mary Shelley dies	

REVISION FOCUS TASK ANSWERS

TASK 1

Walton is a reliable narrator.

- There would seem to be no reason not to trust him. He has no ulterior motive in telling the story in his letters to his sister.
- However, he is egotistical and his vision is limited and perhaps distorted by this.
- He also thinks in very conventional terms and tends to judge on appearances: consider the simple distinctions he makes between Victor (civilised) and monster (primitive).

TASK 2

The monster's fate is determined by his appearance.

- Victor and society generally immediately judge the monster on his appearance.
- Since he is mistreated, he is miserable, and since he is miserable he seeks revenge.
- Nevertheless, he has choices; his life is not completely determined for him. We cannot ignore the fact that he murders the innocent; he could have chosen another path.

TASK 3

As with many Gothic texts, *Frankenstein* challenges set oppositions, in particular the opposition between the monstrous and the human.

- Gothic texts often challenge oppositions such as rational/irrational and civilised/primitive. For example, the characters of Dr Jekyll and Mr Hyde can be seen as parts of the same person.
- Victor defines the creature as monstrous from the start, purely on the basis of his physical appearance, but the creature is initially innocent and benevolent, acting like a monster only once he is rejected and abused by his creator and society.
- The humans in this novel frequently act in monstrous ways. As Elizabeth observes when Justine is executed, 'men appear to me as monsters thirsting for each other's blood' (p. 95).

TASK 4

TVictor's downfall is the result of his search for knowledge.

- Victor's obsession leads him to ignore family and friends.
- Yet perhaps this search for knowledge provides him with an escape from family and friends.
- It may, at any rate, be too simple to assign his downfall purely to his search for knowledge. Other factors – his egotism, for example – are surely involved.

TASK 5

Shelley's monster is a sympathetic figure.

- The monster is initially sympathetic, particularly when we see his loneliness and his desire for love and companionship.
- He is no longer sympathetic when he goes on his murderous rampage.
- In general, the monster may be more sympathetic to the reader than to the characters in the text because we encounter him only through language: we are not literally faced with the full visual horror of the monster.

TASK 6

In *Frankenstein*, the supernatural functions metaphorically to reveal a state of mind.

- The world of the novel is a purely secular world, with no gods and no spirits.
- Victor begins to believe that spirits are watching over him, but this tells us only about his state of mind.
- Could we, however, consider the monster in any way to be a supernatural being? Perhaps we need to define the term clearly before we judge.

MARK SCHEME

Use this page to assess your answer to the Worked task, provided on pages 90–1.

Aiming for an A grade? Fulfil all the criteria below and your answer should hit the mark.*

'Remorse is the dominant feeling expressed by the monster in the final chapter of *Frankenstein*.' Do you agree with this statement or do you think that remorse is tempered by continuing anger and bitterness?

ASSESSMENT OBJECTIVES	MEANING
A01 Articulate creative, informed and relevant responses to literary texts, using appropriate terminology and concepts, and coherent, accurate written expression.	• You make a range of clear, relevant points about remorse, anger and bitterness. • You write a balanced essay covering both positions. • You use a range of literary terms correctly, e.g. **foreshadowing, closure, protagonist, theme, imagery, intertextuality, Romantic, Gothic**. • You write a clear introduction, outlining your thesis and provide a clear conclusion. • You signpost and link your ideas about remorse, anger and bitterness.
A02 Demonstrate detailed critical understanding in analysing the ways in which structure, form and language shape meanings in literary texts.	• You explain the techniques and methods Shelley uses to present remorse, anger and bitterness and link them to main themes of the text. • You may discuss, for example, the ways in which the description of the monster hanging over Victor's coffin echoes the painting of Caroline Beaufort and her father or the moment in which Victor hangs over the body of Elizabeth; the ways in which the monster's expressions of remorse may remind us of those of Victor; images of fire and ice and how they may be linked to remorse and anger. • You explain in detail how your examples affect meaning, e.g. the way in which the monster repeatedly links himself to Milton's Satan might emphasise the continuing conflict between remorse and bitterness. • You may explore how the setting – the barren and icy Arctic wasteland – contributes to the presentation of remorse and bitterness.
A03 Explore connections and comparisons between different literary texts, informed by interpretations of other readers.	• You make relevant links between remorse and bitterness, noting how the expression of the former is undermined by the expression of the latter. • When appropriate, you compare remorse, anger and bitterness in the course of the novel with the presentation of remorse, anger and bitterness in other text(s), e.g. Heathcliff's reactions to Catherine's death. • You incorporate and comment on critics' views of remorse, anger and bitterness are presented in the novel. • You assert your own independent view clearly.
A04 Demonstrate understanding of the significance and influence of the contexts in which literary texts are written and received.	You explain how relevant aspects of social, literary and historical contexts of *Frankenstein* are significant when interpreting expressions of remorse, anger and bitterness. For example, you may discuss: • Literary context: the monster, just like Victor, presents himself in the role of the isolated and alienated Romantic hero-villain. • Historical context: the monster on one level embodies revolutionary violence and is linked to the French Revolution – his anger is partly a protest against injustice. • Social context: the monster's anger is partly the result of his being denied family and friends, and the cult of domesticity is therefore a topic which could be addressed.

* This mark scheme gives you a broad indication of attainment, but check the specific mark scheme for your paper/task to ensure you know what to focus on.